THE LAST GIRLFRIEND ON EARTH

Also by Simon Rich

What in God's Name

Elliot Allagash

Free-Range Chickens

Ant Farm

THE LAST GIRLFRIEND ON EARTH

And Other Love Stories

SIMON RICH

A REAGAN ARTHUR BOOK

LITTLE, BROWN AND COMPANY

NEW YORK BOSTON LONDON

The characters and events in this book are fictitious. Any similarity to real persons, living or dead, is coincidental and not intended by the author.

Reagan Arthur Books / Little, Brown and Company
Hachette Book Group
237 Park Avenue, New York, NY 10017
reaganarthurbooks.com

First Edition: January 2013

Reagan Arthur Books is an imprint of Little, Brown and Company, a division of Hachette Book Group, Inc. The Reagan Arthur Books name and logo are trademarks of Hachette Book Group, Inc.

Illustrations by Matthew Schoch

Portions of this book have appeared, in slightly different form, in *The New Yorker* ("Unprotected," "I Love Girl," "Center of the Universe," and "Trade") and Funny or Die, Inc.'s, e-magazine, *The Occasional* ("Dog Missed Connections").

Library of Congress Cataloging-in-Publication Data
Rich, Simon.
The last girlfriend on earth : and other love stories / Simon Rich. — 1st ed.
p. cm.
ISBN 978-0-316-21939-6
I. Title.
PS3618.I33353L37 2013
813'.6—dc23 2012020337

10 9 8 7 6 5 4 3 2 1

RRD-C

Printed in the United States of America

For Kathleen

Contents

BOY MEETS GIRL

Unprotected

I.

I born in factory. They put me in wrapper. They seal me in box. Three of us in box.

In early days, they move us around. From factory to warehouse. From warehouse to truck. From truck to store.

One day in store, boy human sees us on shelf. He grabs us, hides us under shirt. He rushes outside.

He goes to house, runs into bedroom, locks door. He tears open box and takes me out. He puts me in wallet.

I stay in wallet long, long time.

This is story of my life inside wallet.

II.

The first friend I meet in wallet is Student ID Jordi Hirschfeld. He is card. He has been around longest, he says. He introduces me to other cards. I meet Learner Permit Jordi Hirschfeld, Blockbuster Video Jordi Hirschfeld, Jamba Juice Value Card, GameStop PowerUp Card Jordi Hirschfeld, business card Albert Hirschfeld DDS, Scarsdale Comic Book Explosion Discount Card.

In middle of wallet, there live dollars. I am less close to them, because they are always coming and going. But they are mostly nice. I meet many Ones and Fives, some Tens, a few Twenties. One time, I meet Hundred. He stay for long time. Came from birthday card, he said. Birthday card from an old person.

I also meet photograph of girl human. Very beautiful. Eyes like Blockbuster Video. Blue, blue, blue.

When I first get to wallet, I am "new guy." But time passes. I stay for so long, I soon become veteran. When I first meet Jamba Juice, he has just two stamps. Next thing I know, he has five stamps—then six, then seven. When he gets ten stamps he is gone. One day, Learner Permit disappears. In his place, there is new guy, Driver License. I become worried. Things are changing very fast.

Soon after, I am taken out of wallet. It is night. I am scared. I do not know what is happening. Then I see girl human. She is one from photograph. She looks same in real life, except now she wears no shirt. She is smiling, but when she sees me, she becomes angry. There is arguing. I go back inside wallet.

A few days later, picture of girl human is gone.

III.

That summer, I meet two new friends. The first is Student ID New York University Jordi Hirschfeld. The second is MetroCard.

MetroCard is from New York City and he never lets you forget it. He has real "attitude." He is yellow and black with Cirque du Soleil advertisement on back.

When MetroCard meets GameStop PowerUp Card Jordi Hirschfeld, he looks at me and says, No wonder Jordi Hirschfeld not yet use you. I become confused. Use me for what?

That night, MetroCard tells me many strange things about myself. At first I do not believe what he says. But he insists all is true. When I start to panic, he laughs. He says, What did you think you were for? I am too embarrassed to admit truth, which is that I thought I was balloon.

It is around this time that we move. For more than two years, we had lived inside Velcro Batman. It is nice, comfy. One day, though, without warning, we are inside stiff brown leather. I am very upset—especially when I see that so many friends are gone.

No more GameStop PowerUp Card Jordi Hirschfeld. No more Blockbuster Video Jordi Hirschfeld. No more Scarsdale Comic Book Explosion Discount Card.

Only survivors are MetroCard, Driver License, Student ID, myself, and a creepy new lady named Visa.

I am angry. What was wrong with Velcro Batman? It had many pockets and was warm. I miss my friends and I am lonely.

A few days later, I meet Film Forum Membership Jordan Hirschfeld.

At this point, I am in "panic mode." What is "Film Forum"? Who is "Jordan Hirschfeld"?

Jordan Hirschfeld is same guy as Jordi Hirschfeld, MetroCard explains. He is just trying to "change his image." I am confused. What is wrong with old image? That night, I poke my head out of wallet and look around pocket. It is dark, but I can see we have new neighbor. He says his name is Cigarettes Gauloises. He is very polite, but I get "weird vibe" from him.

It is about this time that I meet strip of notebook paper. On him is written rachelfeingold@nyu.edu.

Now we're getting somewhere, MetroCard says.

I have never been more frightened in my life.

IV.

That Saturday, five crisp Twenties show up. I assume they will stay long time, like most Twenties. But two hours later, they are gone, replaced by receipt La Cucina.

MetroCard looks at receipt La Cucina and laughs. She better put out after *that,* he says. I am confused and worried.

Later on, I am minding my own business, when Jordi (sorry, "Jordan") shoves his finger into me. I am terrified. What was that, I ask. MetroCard grins. He is checking to make sure you're there, he says. For later.

My friends try to calm me down. One of the dollars, a One, tells me about the time he met Vending Machine Pepsi. He was stuffed in and out, in and out, so many times. He almost died. I know he is trying to make me feel better, but I am like, please stop talking about that.

Eventually, the moment comes. It is like other time. I am taken out of wallet and tossed on bed. It is very dark. I can make out shape of girl.

She picks me up and squints at me for a while. Then she turns on lamp.

I am confused. So is Jordan Hirschfeld.

"What's wrong?" he asks.

His face is like Jamba Juice Value Card. Red, red, red.

"I think," she says, "that this might actually be expired."

There is long silence.

And then, all of a sudden, the humans are laughing! And then the girl is hitting Jordan with pillow! And he is hitting her back with pillow! And they are laughing, laughing, laughing.

The girl reaches into her bag.

"Don't worry," she says. "I've got one."

Part of me kind of wants to watch what happens next. But I am quickly covered in pile of clothes.

V.

When I wake up next day, Jordan is dangling me over trash can. I look down into pit. Inside are Cigarettes Gauloises and Film Forum Schedule. They are talking "philosophy." I sigh. I do not really want to move in with them, but what can I do? I figure this is "end of the line" for me.

Suddenly, though, Jordan carries me away—to other side of room. I am placed inside shoe box under his bed.

At first, I am afraid, because it is dark, but as vision adjusts I see I am not alone. There is strip of notebook paper rachelfeingold@nyu.edu. There is receipt La Cucina, on which is now written, "first date."

I spend long, long time in shoe box.

When I arrive, I am "new guy." But as time passes, I become veteran. I welcome many new friends: Birthday card Rachel. Happy Valentine's Day Rachel. And many, many Post-it Notes Rachel. I love you, Jordi. Rachel. Good morning, Jordi! Rachel. Everything in here is Rachel.

I do not know how things are in wallet these days. But I am glad to be in shoe box. I feel as if I have "made it." I am happy. I am warm. I am safe.

Magical Mr. Goat

OLIVIA FROWNED AT HER Marmite sandwich. She knew she must consume it or face the wrath of her governess. But the smell was so revolting she could not bring herself to take a single bite.

She opened the curtains and sighed. It was only teatime, but it might as well have been night. The fog obscured all traces of the sun. It had been raining for days and the entire estate had turned a greyish brown. Even the flower garden had lost its colour. It looked to Olivia like a giant heap of Marmite, mucky and ugly and foul.

"Oh, what a dreadful summer!" she cried.

And indeed it was. Her parents had gone on a three-month pleasure cruise and left her under the care of Ms. Higginberry, a horrid old woman who was constantly forcing her to practice sums. As far as Olivia knew, she was the only child in all of Hamptonshire. There was no one to play with and absolutely nothing to do.

"If only something exciting would happen," she thought miserably. "Anything at all."

She was about to try the loathsome Marmite sandwich when something peculiar caught her eye.

"Good heavens!" she whispered. "Have I gone mad?"

She knew it was impossible, but there appeared to be someone standing in her looking glass.

Olivia was frightened, but she had always been a curious and intrepid child. She stood up slowly and turned to face the mirror.

There—framed in the looking glass—was a large brown goat. He looked like the ones she'd spied on the servants' farm. Two brown horns protruded from his knobby head, and a shaggy beard hung fuzzily from his chin. But unlike most goats, he was standing on his hind legs—and wearing a three-piece suit.

"My goodness!" Olivia gasped. "A goat in a waistcoat!"

"I got it on Jermyn Street," the creature replied. "Isn't it stupendous?"

Olivia began to feel faint.

"You can talk?"

"Yes," the creature confirmed. "But I'm afraid we don't have time for conversation. You see, I've come to take you on an adventure—a stupendous, tremendous one!"

Olivia flushed.

"But my governess... she said I was supposed to sit right here until I finish all my Marmite!"

"Your governess is a Willy Wally! If she fancies Marmite so much, she can eat it herself!"

Olivia laughed for the first time in weeks.

"Why, you're delightful!" she said.

The goat bowed modestly.

"You're too kind."

He stuck his paw through the looking glass, grabbed the Marmite sandwich off her plate, and gobbled it up in a single bite.

"Zerkity zerks!" he said, grimacing. "That was awful! But at least it's gone now—and we can be on our way."

"But where are we going?" Olivia asked her new friend.

The magical creature laughed heartily.

"Where *aren't* we going?"

The next few days were a flurry of excitement. Yes, there were still sums to solve and Marmite sandwiches to eat. But with Mr. Goat by her side, Olivia was happy for the first time all summer. Every afternoon, when Ms. Higginberry took her nap, the wonderful creature leapt through the looking glass and took Olivia on a rollicking adventure. One day, they crept into the pantry and stole sugar cubes from a cupboard. On another outing, they found wagon grease in the basement and oiled up the banister, transforming it into a pleasure slide.

"Stupendous!" Mr. Goat howled as he rocketed down the staircase.

"Tremendous!" Olivia cried, following close behind.

On Saturday, the sun came out, bathing Olivia's bedroom with golden light.

"Zerkity zerks!" Mr. Goat cried. "What a wonderful, sun-derful day!"

He got on all fours and Olivia hopped on his back.

"Giddyup!" she cried.

"At your service, milady!"

She laughed as he barreled down the staircase and out the door, galloping willy-nilly across the grass. After a time, they collapsed in a meadow at the edge of the estate. They lay on the soft earth, laughing uproariously amid the wildflowers.

"Oh, Mr. Goat!" Olivia cried. "The last few days have been ever so much fun!"

"They've been wondrous!" her friend agreed. "Wondrous, fundrous, scrumdrous!"

"I'm so happy you're by my side!"

Mr. Goat leaned in and kissed her.

"Whoa," Olivia said. "Whoa.... What was *that?*"

Mr. Goat flushed with embarrassment.

"I—I'm sorry...," he stammered. "I thought...you know...I thought that's where this was going."

"Well, you thought wrong," Olivia said. "We're just friends. Okay?"

"Okay," Mr. Goat mumbled.

There was a long, awkward pause.

"We should go back," Olivia said, avoiding eye contact.

"Okay," Mr. Goat said.

They walked back to the house in silence.

Olivia was hoping that Mr. Goat would stay away for a few days, so that things could cool down. But the very next day, in the middle of Ms. Higginberry's nap, he popped out of her looking glass.

"Hello, Mr. Goat!" Olivia said cheerfully. She had decided that the best course of action was to pretend nothing strange had happened.

"I fancy an adventure," she said. "How about you?"

"Yeah," Mr. Goat said, clearly distracted. "Yeah."

He coughed nervously. His breath, Olivia noticed, smelled of sherry.

"Listen," he said. "About yesterday..."

"We don't need to talk about that."

"I've been on medication for an ear infection... and the dose was really strong—"

She waved her hand, mercifully cutting him off.

"You don't need to explain," she said. "It's not a big deal. We were friends before yesterday and we're still friends now."

"Well, that's splendid!" Mr. Goat said. "As long as we preserve our friendship—that's the important thing."

"Yes!" Olivia said. "Exactly!"

There was a pause.

"Can I kiss you?" Mr. Goat said.

Olivia groaned.

"I just want to be friends," she said firmly. "That's *all*."

"I know," Mr. Goat said. "I know. I just—I think we should give this thing a try! I mean, there's obviously something between us! You said it yourself, when we were frolicking—you said you wanted me by your side."

"Yeah, like in a 'friend' way."

Mr. Goat growled.

"You led me on."

"What?" Olivia cried. "No, I didn't!"

"You totally led me on! You rode on my back! Do you realize what that was like for me? It was torture! I'm a full-grown goat. I have needs. Stupendous, *tremendous* needs."

"That's not my problem."

Mr. Goat sat down on the floor, massaging his temples with his paws.

"Zerkity zerks," he said. "Zerkity, zerkity zerks."

"Are you going to calm down?" Olivia said. "Because if you're not, I think you should go back through the looking glass."

"I'm sorry," Mr. Goat said. "I'll calm down. I'm sorry."

He smoothed out his suit and took a deep breath.

"So you're not attracted to me at all."

"Mr. Goat—"

"Just tell me. I need to hear you say it. It's the only way I can move on."

Olivia threw up her hands in frustration.

"Okay, fine," she said. "I'm not attracted to you at all."

Mr. Goat burst into tears.

"Oh my God!" he cried. "Oh my God!"

Olivia sighed.

"There, there," she said, patting him halfheartedly on the horns. "You'll find someone."

"That's not true!"

"Sure it is."

"No, it's not! You're the only one who can even *see* me!"

Olivia hesitated. He had a point there.

"Look," she said. "We're great as friends . . . but we're just not physically compatible. I mean, for goodness' sake, I'm only nine years old."

"So what? I'm only eight!"

"Well, yeah, but what is that in goat years?"

Mr. Goat looked down guiltily at his feet.

"It's like midfifties, isn't it?" Olivia said.

Mr. Goat clapped his hooves sarcastically.

"Looks like someone's been practicing her sums."

"You're such a dick," Olivia said. "Just because I'm not giving you what you want, that doesn't give you the right to be a jerk."

"You're right," Mr. Goat mumbled. "I'm sorry."

"I think you'd better leave."

"Okay."

There was another pause—the longest one yet.

"Can I just lick your face one time?" Mr. Goat asked. "Just one time and then I'll go away forever."

"No," Olivia said.

"Please."

"No."

Mr. Goat hung his head and trudged wearily across the nursery. It seemed to Olivia that he was moving as slowly as possible. Eventually, after an interminable length of time, he stepped through the looking glass and vanished. Olivia sighed with relief and sat down by the window. The rain had started up again and the sky was thick with fog.

"Oh," she muttered. "What a dreadful summer."

Occupy Jen's Street

"THE FAT CATS ARE GETTING richer and richer!" Otto screamed hoarsely into his megaphone. "While the genocide rages on! If that's not an injustice, I don't know what is!"

There were only about a dozen protestors left, but they followed along passionately, waving their cardboard signs in the frigid November air. It was freezing out and I was amazed that anyone had come at all. It was a testament to Otto's leadership skills. Every Saturday, regardless of the weather, he got us to follow him to Washington Square Park. We knew, analytically, that our protests were irrational. How could a pack of unwashed college students convince Congress to end the War on Terror, or abolish the American prison system, or legalize hallucinogens? Still, standing there in the cold, with Otto's guttural screams pounding into our skulls, we felt strangely powerful. We felt like we could change whatever we wanted.

"Darfur is a contemporary holocaust!" Otto screeched. "And if we don't stop it, no one will!"

He continued his diatribe, specks of spittle flying everywhere. Suddenly, though, in the middle of the word "industrial-military," his voice trailed off.

"What's wrong?" I asked.

He didn't respond, but I could figure it out by following his forlorn gaze. Jen was strolling across the park, holding hands with a broad-shouldered man in a cardigan. Otto squinted at the pair with rage, his hands trembling slightly at his sides. He'd been screaming for the past four hours, but this was the angriest he'd looked all day.

"If that's not an injustice," he seethed, "I don't know what is."

Otto could be extremely convincing. During our sophomore year, he'd persuaded me to boycott McDonald's, even though they'd recently brought back the McRib. But no matter how hard he tried, he hadn't been able to get Jen to date him.

"It's morally and ethically reprehensible," he said, staring bitterly at Jen's Facebook profile. "I've put in months of labor. How could she enter into a relationship with someone else?"

I nodded sympathetically. It *was* unfair. Otto had been obsessively courting Jen since freshman orientation. He tried to sit with her at every meal. And if her table had no space, he would sit as close to her as possible and look in her direction whenever he made a loud point. He invited her personally to all of his protests. But so far, she hadn't attended a single one. Once, on a Saturday night, I walked in on Otto weeping in the common room. He said it had to do with a situation in Kabul. But I had a feeling it had to do with Jen.

Otto didn't seem sad tonight, though. Just angry.

"It's outrageous," he muttered through gritted teeth. "She refuses to go on a single date with me. Meanwhile, the fat cats on Wall Street just sit there, getting richer and richer."

I was confused.

"What do the fat cats have to do with Jen?"

"It's all connected," he said vaguely.

He grabbed a fresh placard from a stack on his desk and started writing on it with a Sharpie.

"What are you doing?" I asked nervously.

"What does it look like?" he said. "I'm taking a fucking stand."

I passed Otto the next day on my way to Anthro I. He was sitting on the steps of Jen's dormitory, holding his new sign. DATE OTTO NOW, it read, in neatly printed block letters.

"How long have you been out here?" I asked.

"Since last night," he said. "And I'm staying for as long as it takes."

I noticed an open backpack by his side, stuffed with PowerBars and what looked like a first aid kit.

"I don't know if this is such a good idea," I said. "I mean, what are you going to do if it rains?"

"I've got a poncho."

"What about if you have to go to the bathroom?"

"I haven't figured that out yet," he admitted.

"Well... don't you think that's a concern?"

He paused.

"It's a concern," he said.

I looked up at Jen's dormitory. She lived in a twenty-story high-rise at Twelfth and Broadway. I didn't know which apartment was hers, so I couldn't tell if she was even home.

"I should probably go to class," I said apologetically.

"Go ahead," he said. "I'll be right here."

I called Otto from Bobst Library a few hours later. He only had so many PowerBars in his backpack, and I was worried about him. It took a few tries to reach him.

"Sorry," he said. "I was in the Porta Potti."

"Porta Potti? How did you get one of those?"

"One of my volunteers called the city."

"Volunteers?"

He tried to explain, but his voice was drowned out by a thundering sound.

"Gotta go!" he cried out over the din. "Drum circle!"

By the following morning, there were dozens of students on Jen's steps, chanting and banging bongos.

Whose Jen? Otto's Jen!

The crowd was predominantly male, but I was surprised to notice some women there as well. Otto's cause had struck a chord with everyone.

I tried to make my way toward him, but it was difficult to fight through the crowd and eventually I gave up. As I was leaving, a squirrelly-looking guy in a Phish T-shirt handed me a flyer.

OCCUPY JEN'S STREET DEMANDS:

1) Jen must sever ties with her current boyfriend and enter immediately into a long-term sexual relationship with Otto Jankaloff.
2) She must, effective at once, begin to feel love toward him.
3) She must become attracted to him physically.
4) A general reduction in student loans.

I suspected that Otto only threw in the last demand to get more people to his protest. Still, it was an impressive list. Simple, but firm.

The first media reports were dismissive, but as the days went by, they grew increasingly sympathetic. A few celebrities had turned up on the picket line—Alec Baldwin, Yoko Ono—and it had raised the movement's profile.

One night, New York One devoted an entire segment to the Occupy Jen's Street movement. I was surprised to see that the spokesman they interviewed wasn't Otto but an earnest young editor from the *Nation*.

"It's not just about Jen," he said. "It's about the entire romantic system. Ninety-nine percent of men are in love with the top one percent of women. And yet they often refuse to date us. It's a complete injustice."

I started to get worried; Otto's protest was clearly gaining strength, but it seemed to be getting off message.

I tried to talk to Otto the next morning, but it was difficult to find him. An entire tent city had been erected on Jen's street, along with a kitchen and a makeshift stage. I recognized a few members of the Roots setting up equipment. I'd read on the Internet they were going to perform, but I was still surprised to see them.

I found Otto in line for one of the Porta Potties.

"How'd you get the Roots to play?" I asked.

"They just showed up," he said.

Behind us, a cheer rose up from the crowd. Questlove had taken the stage.

"This one's for Oliver!" he said as people cheered.

Otto didn't seem to notice the gaffe. He was jittery from coffee and his beady eyes looked wild. I hoped, for his sake, that things would end soon. One way or another.

By its fifth week, the movement had gone national, with sympathy protests springing up on campuses across the country. Some of the demonstrations had turned violent. At the University of Mississippi, six students were teargassed. (The incident was blamed on "poor officer training.") At NYU, kids were skipping lectures in protest of Jen. Few professors complained; some even joined their students on the streets.

The most dramatic moment came six weeks into the movement. Jen had been avoiding the front entrance to her dormitory for some time. But one day, the back entrance was closed for construction and she had no choice but to cross the picket line. She was with her boyfriend (who turned out to be a mild-mannered rower for the Columbia varsity crew team). The NYPD had given them six full-time security guards, and they all had their hands on their nightsticks. It was a tense moment. The officers cleared a path through the crowd as the couple made their way to the door. They were almost inside when Jen brazenly reached for her boyfriend's hand. No one knows who started the chant, but it lasted for over an hour.

"Shame on you! Shame on you!"

Later that day, NPR broadcast an audio recording of the outburst. It was hard to listen to — visceral and raw.

The protest quickly entered the mainstream. Brian Williams devoted an hour to the movement, and the other anchors followed suit. It was an election year, and before long politicians had no choice but to pay lip service to the cause.

"There's obviously a lot of rage right now," the president said at a press conference. "A lot of rage toward Jen."

Ten weeks into the protest, Jen held a press conference of her own. On the advice of counsel, she'd agreed to go out with Otto, once, for coffee. It was a major victory for the movement, obviously, but Otto wasn't satisfied. She still hadn't budged on any of the major issues. She refused to end her relationship with her current boyfriend. And while she'd agreed to "meet up for coffee," she had pointedly stopped short of calling it a date.

"I think you should take it," I told Otto the next time I saw him. His clothes were stiff with sweat and dirt and his beard looked filthier than ever. But his confidence had only intensified. At some point, he'd begun to wear a beret.

"I'm not backing down," he said. "Not when I'm this close."

A few weeks later, a blizzard hit New York, burying it in over a foot of snow. Within a couple of days, almost everyone had left the encampment on Jen's street. The only people who remained were Otto and a few elderly Native American people, who looked like they might be homeless. One day, a few haggard men from the Industrial Workers of the World showed up. Otto was thankful for their presence at first. He was running out of followers and needed all the support he could get. But he soon found out they had started holding meetings without him. One morning, on my way to class, I saw them dismantling what remained of his encampment.

"Stop!" Otto shrieked at them, his voice thick and phlegmy. "What are you doing?"

"Didn't you hear?" a grizzled organizer told him. "It's over. We won."

Otto's eyes widened.

"Seriously? She's going to date me?"

The organizer shook his head.

"We couldn't get her to budge on that," he said. "But she agreed to let us use her bathroom."

He gestured at the other union guys, who were forming a single-file line in front of Jen's steps.

"You want to get in line?" the organizer asked him. "We each get two minutes."

Otto shook his head. His eyes, I noticed, were glossy with tears. He'd lost weight during the protest and was now only slightly overweight. I put an arm around his shoulder and walked him back to his dorm. It was hard to believe it was all over.

I finished college, went to business school, and got a job as a consultant. At some point I lost touch with Otto. I never went to a protest again.

I still believe that change is possible. With enough hard work and organization, there's no reason activists can't stop genocide, achieve nuclear disarmament, eradicate poverty, or end all human wars. But when it comes to the stuff that really matters, the stuff that really counts? There's nothing you can do.

Dog Missed Connections

m4w—East River Dog Run

Saw you at the dog run yesterday morning. You were wearing a leather collar and running around in circles. I was wearing a gold collar and trying to have sex with you. At one point I managed to mount you and we sort of had sex for a couple of seconds. You shook me off, though, and ran away. I'm interested in getting to know you a little better. We obviously have chemistry and even though we just met once I really sensed a connection. I'll be back at the dog run tomorrow morning. Hope to see you there.

m4w—FDR Drive

I saw you out the window of my master's car during a traffic jam. We barked at each other for a while. I thought you made some interesting points. Would love to meet up sometime for a casual, low-key date. Maybe we could go to Central

Park together and eat garbage off the ground. Open to anything.

m4w—75th Street and Park Avenue

Spotted you yesterday afternoon, helping a blind human cross the street. I can tell you've got a gentle soul and a caring heart. Would love to mount you violently from behind and have aggressive sex with your body.

w4m—Astoria, alley behind Taco Bell

Saw you by the Dumpster, eating a pile of what appeared to be human vomit. You seemed like someone who doesn't take himself too seriously. Not sure if you're male or female, but either way I'd love to smell your genitals. Let me know if you're intrigued.

m4w—83rd and Broadway

Saw you a few hours ago, tied to a parking meter outside Zabar's. You had a large cone on your head and seemed frustrated. Life's too short for drama. I think you're cute. Let's meet up sometime and forget about our worries for a while. :)

I am neutered, BTW, but no one ever complains. . . .

m4w—Chelsea Dog Run

Noticed you at the Chelsea dog run last night. You were wearing a red sweater and nothing else. We sniffed each other's genitals for a while and I was about to have sex with you when another dog came over and starting having sex with *me*, even though I am a male. By the time I escaped from him you were gone. It really felt like a lost opportunity. Would love to meet up sometime and continue where we left off.

m4w—living room

I saw you recently in my master's house, dangling over the side of a couch. You were a long, fleshy tube with a knee in the middle and a sneaker at the end. I tried to hump you, but you kicked me away. Listen: I know you're a leg. And who knows if you'll even read this. But for what it's worth, I just wanted to say I think you're beautiful.

Sirens of Gowanus

BRENT WAS WALKING HOME from band practice when he heard a girl singing. He recognized the song immediately; it was that new Arcade Fire song, his favorite track off their new album. He put down his amp and listened as she belted out the chorus. It was a busy night on Smith Street but her crisp, clear voice pierced easily through the clatter.

He heaved his amp over his shoulder and headed toward the singer. She had moved on to another tune by now—a b-side by Big Star. The streetlamps grew sparser as he neared the Gowanus Canal, but he was able to spot her in the moonlight. She was under the Carroll Street bridge, sitting on a round, smooth rock. Her silky eyelashes fluttered as she sang. And whenever she hit a high note, she playfully splashed the water with her feet. She was naked from the waist up, two large breasts protruding from her slender, bird-like frame.

Brent was trying to figure out what to say to her when she called out his name.

"I'm sorry," he said. "Do I know you?"

She bashfully turned away, her pale cheeks crimsoning in the moonlight.

"Not exactly," she said. "But I've been to a couple of your shows. You're in the Fuzz, right?"

Brent's eyes widened with amazement. His band had only formed a few months ago. No one had ever recognized him before. Even when he headlined at Club Trash, he'd had to show his ID at the door.

"I can't believe you've heard of me," he admitted.

The girl let loose a high-pitched musical laugh.

"I haven't just *heard* of you!" she cried. "I *worship* you!"

She took a deep breath and broke into one of his songs—the final track on the Fuzz's self-released EP.

Brent moved closer to the water. He knew the Gowanus Canal was filthy. He'd read once online that its water was so putrid it had somehow tested positive for gonorrhea. But it looked so lovely in the moonlight, a solid strip of blue, weaving elegantly through the city.

Brent talked to her for hours that night—about music and art and "the scene." When the sun started to rise, he gave her his cell phone number and wobbled off toward the F train. He'd barely walked a block when she texted him: "I hope U come back 2morrow!" Brent shook his head, laughing with giddiness. He could hardly believe his luck.

"Dude, that girl's trouble."

Brent scoffed.

"What are you talking about?"

His roommate Rob turned toward him, muting the TV to emphasize his words' importance.

"She's a fucking siren," he said. "She lures people out to that rock and, like, eats their flesh."

Brent rolled his eyes.

"I'm serious," Rob said. "Remember Stanley? The bassist in Dustin's band? She ate his face off."

"You can't judge someone by their past relationships. Like, okay, she killed Stanley. But how do you know what was going on between them? You weren't there. Maybe if you heard Thelxiepeia's take on what happened, you'd side with her."

Rob sighed.

"It's your life," he said. "I just don't want to see you get hurt."

Brent decided to invite her to Bar Tabac. It was a great first-date restaurant: not too expensive but classy enough to show a girl you were trying. It was also convenient—halfway between his apartment and her rock.

"I'd love to see you!" she cooed over the phone. "But I'm not super into French food."

Brent suggested a few alternatives—Thai, Italian, Mexican—but she balked at all of them.

"Where do *you* want to eat?" he asked.

Her breathing grew strangely thick.

"At my place," she said.

Brent couldn't believe it; he'd only known the girl for two days and she was already inviting him over! He called his drummer to cancel band practice. He needed to go buy a swimsuit.

"How's this one?" Brent asked Rob, holding up a purple Speedo.

"If you swim to that rock," he said, "she's going to kill you."

Brent ignored him and turned to his other roommate, Jeff. "What do *you* think?"

"I think you're going to die," Jeff said.

Brent threw up his hands in frustration.

"Why do you guys always have to be so negative?"

"Just tell me this," Jeff said. "That rock she was sitting on. Did you see any bones on it?"

Brent sighed. There had been a few bones.

"Okay," Rob said. "I take it from your silence that you saw bones. Did she say anything about where they came from?"

"I didn't ask," Brent admitted.

"Why not?" Jeff asked.

"I just met her!" Brent said. "I don't know what kind of food issues she has! I didn't want to make her uncomfortable. I'm trying not to blow this."

He walked in silence to the checkout line. How could he explain his situation to those cynical morons? How could he explain the way this beautiful girl made him feel? They'd only met once and he already caught himself daydreaming about their future. He could easily picture them moving in together someday. His apartment was tiny, and so was her rock, but maybe they could find a bigger place? Brent visualized their wedding. They'd have it outside, on the shores of the Gowanus. He was pretty sure Thelxiepeia was a gentile, based on her hair color and the number of times she'd mentioned Zeus. But he didn't care about that kind of stuff.

"Do you need a bag?" the cashier asked him as he paid for his purple Speedo.

"That's okay," Brent said. "I'm going to put it on right now."

Brent hurried toward the water, his roommates both struggling to keep up.

"There's still time to cancel," Jeff said.

"Yeah," Rob said. "Just text her saying you're sick. The three of us can go get wings."

Brent spun around swiftly, his cheeks flushed with rage.

"Look," he said. "I'm not an idiot, okay? I know the odds are against us. I know she's a siren. I know she's eaten people. I know she's five thousand years older than me. But I *really* like her."

His eyes grew moist.

"I think," he said, "I might even be in *love* with her."

Her voice sounded in the distance. She was singing a Magnetic Fields tune—something off 69 *Love Songs*. She was almost up to the chorus when two more voices suddenly joined her. Brent's roommates looked out onto the Gowanus. Apparently, Thelxiepeia had invited some friends over.

"Holy shit," Rob whispered as the three topless girls sang on. "Those girls are hot."

Jeff said nothing; he just stared at the water in silence, his lips slightly parted.

The girls finished singing and waved hello, playfully splashing the water with their feet.

"Are you Rob Swieskowski?" the one on the left asked. "I love your YouTube comedy videos."

Rob blushed.

"I can't believe you've seen those."

"And you're Jeff Selsam!" the other siren interrupted.

"Actuary of the Month at Chapman and Chapman Life Insurance."

Jeff's eyes widened.

"How did you know?"

The sirens nodded at each other and then broke into a Beatles song, their voices braided perfectly in harmony. They smiled at the men, beckoning them closer.

And closer.

Cupid

ZEUS LOOKED AT HIS WATCH.

"Are you sure you told him five o' clock?" he asked.

"Yes," Hermes said. "I'm sure."

"Because it's almost *six*."

"Well, what do you want me to do?" Hermes snapped.

They sat in silence for another fifteen minutes. Finally, Cupid wobbled through the clouds and plopped onto the top of Mount Olympus. He was wearing some kind of hip-hop jumpsuit, with holes cut in the back to accommodate his wings. For a while, Zeus had ignored his grandson's hip-hop obsession, assuming it was just another phase. He'd gone through so many in just the past century. There was his "abstract painter" phase in the 1920s, then his "beat poet" phase in the fifties. His rap phase, though, had lasted longer than both of those combined. It worried Zeus.

"New shit, new shit," Cupid said, handing Zeus a homemade mix CD.

The King of Gods tucked it awkwardly into his robe.

He'd put his grandson in charge of love because it seemed like the cushiest job on Mount Olympus. All you had to do, basically, was fly around and shoot humans with arrows. The more you fired, the more couples would form and the happier mankind would be. Zeus didn't expect Cupid to provide every single mortal with romance. But he figured he'd at least crack the 10 percent mark. Even that modest number, though, seemed too daunting for the young god. In an average day, Cupid only launched about four arrows—and most of them missed their mark. Recently, he'd lost his bow in the back of a New York City taxicab. It was two months before he got around to replacing it. His laziness was astounding. He was supposed to circle the globe three times a day, spreading love to all the peoples of the earth. But in the past five years, he'd barely left Manhattan's Meatpacking District. He didn't even like to try new clubs. According to Hermes, he'd gone to Tenjune eleven nights out of the last twelve.

"Did Hermes tell you why I wished to speak with you?" Zeus asked.

Cupid muttered something in return, but he was using so much contemporary Earth language that Zeus was mystified. The only thing he could make out distinctly was the "N" word.

"I told you I don't like it when you use that word," he said. "It makes me very uncomfortable."

Cupid shrugged.

"I'ma be me," he said.

Zeus cleared his throat. There was no point in waiting any longer; he would just have to come right out and say it.

"Cupid," he said, "I think you need to go back to rehab."

"Nah, Z," Cupid said. "Nah."

"It's obvious your drinking is starting to interfere with your work."

"That's whack," Cupid said. "I've been setting up hella matches."

Zeus sighed. He hadn't spent much time around humans since the time of kings, but even he could sense that Cupid's slang was dated.

"It's not just how few arrows you're firing," he said. "It's who you're firing them at."

"What are you talking about? I always hook up the illest humans."

"Well, then, would you mind explaining your criteria?"

Cupid stared at him blankly, clearly stumped by the word "criteria."

"Just tell me," Zeus pressed on. "How do you decide which humans receive love?"

Cupid reached into his diaper and scratched his groin unselfconsciously.

"Well, with brothers," he said, "it's all about style. You

don't get an arrow unless you're, like, a club promoter or, like, a vodka promoter."

"So just promoters."

Cupid nodded vaguely.

"Okay," Zeus said. "What about women? Which of them receive your arrows?"

"Ones that bring the heat."

"What does that mean?"

Cupid hiccupped.

"Big tits."

Zeus sighed.

"You're drunk right now, aren't you?"

"I got a little lean on," Cupid admitted.

Zeus's eyelids fluttered with impatience.

"So to recap," he said, "the only humans you help are men with 'style' and women who 'bring the heat.'"

Cupid nodded.

"And the rest of the humans . . . the ones, for example, who don't visit upscale dance clubs . . . they're just supposed to fend for themselves?"

Cupid shrugged.

"Not my fault they can't get in anywhere."

Hermes shot Zeus a firm look. The King of Gods cleared his throat and went into the speech he'd rehearsed.

"There's a place in Phoenix called the Sanctuary," he said.

"They specialize in addiction. They can give you all the tools you need to beat this thing. Will you please take this gift of help that I'm offering you today?"

"Nah, Z..."

"Please," Zeus begged. "Mankind is depending on you."

Cupid waved his pudgy arms dismissively.

"Nah," he mumbled. "This whole thing's a setup. I'm outee."

He hopped off the mountain and zigzagged back to Manhattan, his bow and arrow drawn.

"Should I fly after him?" Hermes offered.

Zeus shook his head and sighed.

"It's too late," he said. "We've lost him."

Set Up

I FELT A LITTLE WEIRD asking my friends to set me up. But the sad truth was I was starting to get desperate. I'd been single for so long I'd forgotten how the courtship process even worked. I'd had girlfriends before, in college and graduate school. But I couldn't for the life of me remember how I'd met them. Had I just walked up to them and started talking? Had they just walked up to *me* and started talking? It seemed like a different person's life.

Tim and Tina leapt at the chance to help me. The second I brought up my dating woes they sprang into action, even though it was right in the middle of their engagement party.

"We did some reconnaissance," they told me after circling the living room. "Every woman here is in a relationship."

"Figures," I said.

"Don't worry," Tina said. "We're on the case!"

They grinned at me and I felt a jolt of excitement. Tim and Tina were the two most social people I knew. She was a film publicist with hundreds of clients. He'd just made partner at the largest corporate law firm in Manhattan. If this golden couple couldn't find me a date, no one could.

A few months passed. I was starting to feel hopeless. But then, on a sunny day in April, the phone rang in my Bushwick apartment.

"Guess what?" Tim said. "We found you one."

"Wow! Really?"

"Really," Tina said. "You're on speakerphone, by the way."

"What's she like?"

"She's totally your type," Tim said. "She's confident, super-cute, *completely* hilarious. Oh, and guess where's she from? Sweden."

"Whoa," I said. "That's awesome."

"Come over for brunch," Tina said. "We need to, like, *strategize.*"

I took the L train to the R train to the F train, emerging finally in Carroll Gardens. Tim and Tina had just bought a brownstone on a cozy, tree-lined side street near the water.

"It's a bit on the small side," Tim said modestly. "But it's in an excellent district."

It took me a second to realize he meant "school district." We really were getting old.

Tina emerged from the kitchen with a pitcher of mimosas.

"Okay," she said. "Let's get down to business."

I chuckled nervously and joined them at the dining room table.

"I think the best thing to do is to let it happen naturally," Tim said. "We'll invite her over to brunch next Sunday, sit you guys next to each other, and let you take it from there."

I felt my heart speed up. It was bad enough striking out in bars, where the lights were low and nobody was watching. Did I really want to risk getting rejected in front of my two closest friends?

"Don't worry," Tim said, sensing my anxiety. "She's really excited to meet you."

"Really?"

"We showed her a picture," Tina told me. "She thinks you're cute."

I blushed so intensely that they both started to laugh.

"Oh my God!" Tina said. "This is just like high school!"

"How recent a picture did you show her?" I joked. "Was my bald spot in the shot?"

"She's into bald guys," Tim said. "Her last boyfriend was completely bald."

I heard a knocking sound and realized I was rapping my knuckles against the table. I felt a strange urge to laugh out loud. I was excited, I realized, genuinely excited, for the first time since my thirtieth birthday.

"Do you have a picture of her?" I asked.

Tina chuckled.

"Getting down to brass tacks, huh? Don't worry, I'll go find one."

Tim refilled our mimosa glasses while Tina went upstairs. I assumed she was going to get her laptop, but when she returned, she was holding a short stack of blurry Polaroids.

"Voila!" she said, plopping them down on the table.

I picked up the first one. It was extremely dim. All I could make out was a large, brownish pile of trash.

"Where'd you take this?" I asked.

"In the dump," Tim said casually.

"Where is she?"

Tina pointed to the center of the photograph. I squinted. There, between two black garbage bags, was a hunched, furry figure, covered in red warts.

"Her name is Gorbachaka," Tina said. "With a 'G.'"

I felt my forehead growing damp.

"Something wrong?" Tim asked.

"I guess... she just wasn't what I was expecting."

"What were you expecting?" Tina said, a slight edge to her voice.

"I don't know," I mumbled. "I just, you know... you said she was from Sweden."

"She is," Tina said. "She was born in the Scandinavian

forest. She moved to the States last year so she could live under the Manhattan Bridge."

"Does that mean she's a troll?"

Tina nodded. "Is that a problem?"

"No," I said, trying to be polite. "I just... I guess I'm just not sure she's my type."

Tim and Tina looked at each other with exasperation.

"I'm going to get a glass of water," Tina said. Tim waited until she was gone and then leaned across the table.

"Look, buddy," he said. "You asked us to help you find a date. And we did."

"I know," I said. "And it's really nice of you to put in the effort. I'm just not that attracted to her. I mean, her feet are *so* big. And her teeth look really sharp."

Tim rolled his eyes.

"No offense or anything?" he said. "But I think your standards might be a little bit too high. I know this girl isn't exactly a runway model. But *you're* not exactly..."

He trailed off.

"My point is," he said, "you're not getting any younger. I think it's maybe time you lowered your bar a bit."

"I guess you're right," I said softly.

Tim grinned.

"Tina!" he shouted. "He's in!"

Word of the setup spread among my friends, and over the next few days I was bombarded with phone calls. I even heard from Bill and Becky, who were in the middle of a vacation in Barbados.

"Hey, stud," Bill said. "I heard you got a date lined up."

"Yeah!" I said, trying my best to sound positive.

"I think you two are going to make, like, the cutest couple *ever,*" Becky said. I was apparently on speakerphone again.

"Don't stress," Bill said. "You're going to knock 'er dead."

I knew my friends were trying to be supportive, but there was something about their tone that I found a bit condescending. I knew I wasn't the world's greatest catch. My apartment was small and poorly lit. I'd been a full-time temp since grad school. I was losing hair and gaining weight and I hadn't picked up a girl in over two years. But there was still something inside me, a small prideful voice, telling me I could do better.

Tim swung open the door and grinned at me.

"There he is," he said. "The man of the hour."

I peeked inside and was annoyed to see that Bill and

Becky had been invited along to the brunch, as well as Cait and Chris and Jim and Jenny.

"I thought it was just going to be the four of us," I said.

"Everyone wanted to come and help you out," Tim said. "You can never have too many wingmen, right?"

I reluctantly stepped inside. The couples all waved cheerfully at me. I began to feel anxious, like a child who's been asked to put on a performance for grown-ups.

Tina squealed when she saw me.

"Guess what?" she said in a singsong voice. "She's he-ere!"

I heard her before I saw her. She was in the kitchen, chugging from a pitcher of mimosas. She looked up when I entered, her thick black beard clotted with orange pulp.

"Hi," I said, waving awkwardly.

"Goor!" she shouted. "Gooooor!"

She continued to drink from the pitcher.

"She isn't capable of human speech," Tina explained. "But she's excited to see you."

Gorbachaka kept drinking until the liquid was gone. Then she smashed the glass pitcher on the floor, charged across the kitchen, and bit me on the leg.

"Fuck!" I shouted as her fangs sank into my calf.

Tina laughed.

"I told you," she whispered. "Gorba's *hilarious*."

Tim entered suddenly, a sly grin on his face. Over his

shoulder I could see the rest of my friends, smiling conspiratorially.

"Hey, Tina," Tim said in a stagy voice. "Would you come help me find those, uh . . . napkins?"

My friends all giggled.

"Of course," Tina said, smirking at me and Gorbachaka. "I'll leave *you* two alone."

She left the kitchen and closed the door, sealing us in.

"So," I said, trying my best to make conversation. "How did you meet Tim and Tina?"

"Goor!" Gorbachaka growled.

She tried again to bite me and I leapt out of the way.

"Goor!" she repeated. "GOOOR!"

She lunged at me again and I instinctively kicked her. She was short—about two foot six—and the momentum sent her flying. She crashed into a cabinet, her skull cracking against it like a rock. It looked for a moment like she was dead, but then her yellow eyes shot open. She leapt into a squatting position and charged at me again. I dodged out of the way, and she crashed into the door. It swung wide open, revealing my friends, all of whom had obviously been eavesdropping.

"Is everything okay?" Tina asked.

"No!" I shouted. "It's not!"

Tim pulled me aside.

"Maybe calm down a bit," he whispered. "You're not exactly making the greatest first impression."

"I don't care!" I shouted. "This isn't going to work!"

"Why not?"

"Because she's an ugly fucking troll!"

Everyone gasped. I looked around the room; no one would make eye contact with me.

Tina knelt down so she could look Gorbachaka in the eye.

"Oh my God," she said. "Gorba, I'm so sorry."

Gorbachaka banged her paw against the ground.

"BRAGA BRAGA HUCK!" she screeched.

"I know," Tina said, fixing me with a stare. "He shouldn't have said that."

Tim laid his palm on my shoulder.

"I think you should maybe leave, buddy," he said. "Let this blow over."

I nodded awkwardly and slowly made my way out of their house.

I don't really hang out with my friends much anymore. I call them sometimes on the weekends, to see if they want to hit the bars, but they always seem to be busy, shopping for apartments, or visiting in-laws, or assembling cribs.

I've joined OkCupid, Match.com, and eHarmony—but

none have resulted in any actual dates. Sometimes I think about spicing up my online profile, to try to make myself seem more alluring. But it doesn't seem worth the effort.

Last month, I was flipping through the Sunday *Times* when I saw Gorbachaka's face in the "Vows" section. She'd gotten married at Temple Emanuel, the article said, to an accountant named Jared. He had an MBA from Cornell and was surprisingly attractive. Gorbachaka didn't look too bad herself. She'd lost a few pounds, trimmed her beard, and gotten her fangs whitened. I thought about finding her on Facebook and maybe poking her or something. But then I changed my mind. What was the point? I'd already had my shot, and I had blown it.

Eureka

CHARLES DARWIN REACHED INTO his satchel and extracted a pair of male lizard skeletons. He knew they must be of the same species. And yet they varied dramatically in size and structure. What accounted for their anatomical differences? How had such deviations come to pass? He had been pondering such issues for months now. But despite his assiduous journal-keeping, he had yet to make a breakthrough.

Darwin scratched his sunburnt scalp and sighed. It was extraordinarily hot on the Galapagosian shore, even in the shade of the anchored HMS *Beagle*. He was considering wading into the water when he caught sight of an exquisite creature. It was a native girl. Her flesh was taut and tan and entirely devoid of clothing.

Darwin's cheeks flushed beneath his beard. He had seen drawings of nude women in textbooks during his university days. But he had never seen one "in the flesh," as it were. He was debating whether or not to hide when she casually strolled toward him, her long black hair swaying gently in the equatorial breeze.

"Tanaka?" she asked.

"Pardon?" Charles mumbled. He was struggling desperately to keep his eyes from straying downward, to her lithe, sun-kissed torso.

"Tanaka?" the girl repeated. Charles realized she was pointing at his lizard skeletons.

"Ah!" he said proudly. "They are scientific specimens."

She took the smaller lizard skeleton and squinted at it, turning it over in her small brown hand. Darwin felt a surge of pride. She was interested, evidently, in his work.

"Tanaka," the girl said, handing the lizard back to him.

"Yes!" Darwin said enthusiastically. *"Tanaka!"*

He took the girl's hand and gave it a hearty shake.

"My name is Charles," he said. "I am the ship's naturalist."

He held up his specimens.

"This is the male of the species," he explained. "Over time, its body has grown in size and strength. I'm attempting to discover why."

The girl stared at him blankly, her long black eyelashes fluttering slightly. Darwin began to fear that he was losing her.

"It's quite interesting work," he said. "Here—I'll show you some of my recent data...."

He was fumbling in his satchel for his journal when he heard lumbering footsteps behind him. It was Mac, the ship's boatswain.

"Hey, Chuck," said the sailor. "Who you talking to?"

Darwin forced a smile. He had never particularly gotten along with Mac. In truth, he found the man somewhat barbaric. He rarely wore his shirt to meals. And once he had swiped Darwin's microscope and used it to play "catch" with his mates. Darwin wanted to tell the sailor to leave, but etiquette called for an introduction.

"This is a native girl I met," he said stiffly. "I was just showing her my research."

"I'll take it from here," Mac said.

He picked the girl up and casually tossed her over his shoulder. She giggled as he carried her into the water, her nubile legs kicking playfully against his broad, bare back.

"Tanaka!" she cried, her naked chest heaving with laughter. *"Tanaka!"*

"You're crazy," Mac said, chuckling to himself.

They fell into the water and began to splash each other.

Darwin squinted at the couple—and then back at his two male lizard specimens.

"Oh," he murmured. "Now I get it."

NASA Proposal

Author: Dr. Norman Bergman

Proposed Experiment: To determine the effects of zero gravity on human mating.

Requirements: In order to conduct this experiment, you would have to find a male and a female who currently reside in outer space.

Author Background: I currently reside in outer space, with my colleague Dr. Jessica Mullins, in the Alpha Space Orb. We have resided in this orb for twenty-seven months. We are the only two people in this orb.

Can you think of any individuals who could successfully carry out this experiment? No, not off the top of my head. I've really only thought about this mating experiment in the abstract, as a way to learn about gravity and things.

What obstacles to this experiment can you foresee? None! Really, all you have to do is find two people in outer space who live together, preferably in some kind of pod or orb, and say to them, "We're doing this experiment." They don't have to be married or even particularly well suited for mating. They could have totally different personalities and not even really get along that well. But if you explained to them that they would only be mating as an experiment, for NASA, they would probably be like, "Well, this is pretty strange because we're not even really on speaking terms anymore, but it's an experiment for NASA and we both work for NASA so we should probably just do this experiment one time. After that, who knows, maybe we'll want to keep mating, but right now the important thing is to try it once for science."

Respectfully submitted,

Dr. Norman Bergman
Copilot, Alpha Space Orb

Archaeological Excavation Report: Ludlow Lounge

Introduction

The following report summarizes our findings at the archaeological site known as Ludlow Lounge. Most of our records of Earth 1 were lost in the Great Google Crash of 4081. But all evidence suggests that this structure once served as a ritualistic social hub for primitive, pre-Internet man.

Findings

Not much is known about pre-Internet courtship rituals. But presumably, if a twentieth-century male was in need of sexual release, he had no choice but to physically approach a female and, without any kind of warning, begin speaking to her. Needless to say, this must have been a highly upsetting experience for everyone involved. In order to mitigate the horror of the situation, primitive humans relied on a poison known as beer (figure 1) to damage their brains to the point of near unconsciousness.

Based on the comparative filth of the "Men's" and "Women's" restrooms (figures 2 and 3), we know that males heavily outnumbered females in this location. A sign reading LADIES' NIGHT (figure 4) suggests that males made a primitive effort to lure more females into the space. It is unclear, though, whether this strategy ever met with any success.

One other discovery was a small tin box (figure 5) found near the bar's entrance. The box was filled with paper currency and stamped with the phrase "Friday/Saturday Cover Five Dollars." This box indicates that humans, incredibly, paid money to enter this space and have the kind of experience previously described.

Conclusion

Before OkCupid profiles became mandated by the Galactic Government, the only way to find a mate was to self-induce brain damage and beg strangers for sex in public. The fact that anyone ever achieved sexual congress during these dark times is a remarkable testament to man's will to survive.

Victory

How'd you sleep?" Lydia asked.

"Great," Josh said. "Really, *really* great."

She laughed and bashed his face with a pillow.

"You haven't seen my bra, have you?"

"I think I threw it that way," he said, pointing vaguely across the room. She hopped out of bed, her smooth back shining in the morning sun. Josh shook his head in amazement. Twelve hours ago, he didn't even know this wonderful person. And now here she was, voluntarily naked, inside his bedroom.

"Are you hungry?" he asked. "There's a good brunch place around the corner."

"I wish I could stay," she said, tousling his hair. "But I should get back to Greenpoint. My roommate's probably pretty worried about me."

She blushed. "I don't usually do this sort of thing."

Josh squeezed her hand. "Me neither."

He spotted her bag beneath some pillows and handed it to

her. She smiled at him gratefully and slung it over her shoulder.

"Sorry the place is such a mess," he said as he led her down the hallway.

"It's okay," she said. "You didn't know you were going to have company."

He laughed and kissed her tentatively on the cheek.

"So," he said. "Do you want to maybe hang out again sometime?"

She grinned at him.

"That would be great."

He kissed her again, more confidently this time, and then opened the door for her.

"See ya soon!" she said.

"Yeah!" he said. "See ya."

He was almost back to his bedroom when his cell phone started ringing. He extracted it from his crumpled jeans and checked the screen. It was an unlisted number, but he decided to answer anyway.

"Hello?"

"I hear congratulations are in order."

Josh chuckled.

"Hello, Mr. President."

"I'm calling to pay tribute to your achievements," said the

commander in chief. "You are an inspiration to men everywhere."

"Wow, thanks," Josh said. "That's really nice of you to say."

"I mean it," the president said. "It takes incredible courage to approach an attractive girl at a bar and begin speaking with her. And the fact that you were able to convince her to go back to your apartment, and have relations with you, is extraordinary."

Josh blushed. He knew the president was only phoning him because of protocol. Still, he couldn't help feeling touched by the man's words.

"It's so cool of you to call," he said. "I'm honored."

"Are you kidding?" the president said. "The honor is all mine."

Josh heard some commotion on the other end of the line. It sounded like the president's aides were trying to get his attention.

"Who?" he heard the president whisper. "The generals? Tell them they can wait. I'm talking to Josh."

Josh put the president on speakerphone so he could clean up his bedroom while they spoke.

"I still can't believe you really did it," the president said.

"Neither can I!" Josh said, as he tossed a condom wrapper

in the trash. "I mean, I've never done it before. Just, like, picked up a girl at a bar."

"I've come close," the president volunteered. "Like this one time, in law school, I was at a bar and I saw this girl I knew from section. And we went home together that night."

"That's different, though," Josh said. "Because you already knew her."

"I know," the president said. "It's different. Also, we didn't go all the way. We just made out."

Josh's phone began to beep.

"Hold on one sec," he said. "I've got another call."

"I'll hold," the president said.

Josh glanced at his phone's screen. It was another unlisted number. He shrugged and clicked Accept.

"Hello?"

"Good morning, Joshua!" replied an elderly-sounding Englishman. "I'm calling from the MacArthur Foundation. I'm pleased to announce that you will be receiving one of our annual awards."

"You mean the 'genius' grant?"

The Englishman chuckled.

"That's how it's known colloquially, yes," he said. "Where shall we send the five-hundred-thousand-dollar check?"

Josh gave him the address of his apartment.

"Listen," he said. "I'm sorry, but I should probably go. I've got the president on the other line."

"Of course," the Englishman said. "But before you hang up, would you mind clarifying something for me?"

"Sure," Josh said. "What's up?"

"The MacArthur board members were all wondering... how exactly did you do it?"

"Do what?"

"Seal the deal with Lydia. Did you, like, use a 'line'?"

Josh thought about it.

"Well, when I first saw her, she was picking a song on the jukebox. So I walked over to her and said, 'Nice pick.'"

"And then what? The conversation just proceeded from there?"

"Well, no—I wanted to play it cool. So after that thing at the jukebox I walked back to where my friends were sitting."

Josh heard a scribbling noise over the phone; the Englishman was taking notes. Josh paused for a moment to give him a chance to catch up.

"...walked back...to where your friends...were seated. Yes, all right. Got it."

"So, anyway," Josh said. "Like, twenty minutes after the thing at the jukebox, I saw that she was getting another drink. So I walked over to the bar. And I kind of, like, timed it so that we'd bump into each other."

The scribbling stopped; the man sighed heavily into the receiver.

"Genius," he said.

"Thanks," Josh said. "Hey, out of curiosity, who else got grants this year?"

"Oh, the usual. Cancer doctors and whatnot. So, okay, you're standing next to her at the bar. Then what?"

"Well, then we just started talking."

"About what?"

"Lots of stuff. We're both studying for the GREs, so we talked about that for a while. And, you know, our favorite iPhone apps and stupid things like that. She seemed really cool."

"And how'd you get her to come back to your place? What did you say?"

"Well, we had been talking about this TV show *Gold Rush,* and how funny it was, so I said, 'Want to come over and watch an episode of *Gold Rush*?' "

"Unbelievable."

"Yeah," Josh said. "It was great."

"What's her full name?"

Josh gave it to him.

"Okay, hold on, I'm Googling her."

Josh waited patiently.

"Whoa. She's cute."

"I know," Josh said. "Listen, I've got the president on the other line still..."

"Oh, right! I'll let you go."

"Thanks again for the five hundred thousand dollars."

"Of course."

Josh switched back to the president.

"Sorry about that," he said.

"Not a problem," the president said. "So how'd you leave it with her? Are you going to see her again?"

"I hope so. She said she wanted to, so I'll probably call her the next time I'm free."

"You don't want to call her too soon," the president warned. "You want to wait, like, a day or—"

He cut himself off.

"Look at me," he said, chuckling self-consciously. "Giving *you* advice."

Josh's phone buzzed again. He checked the screen and laughed.

"Oh, man!" he said. "It's her, she's on the other line."

"Take it!" the president shouted. "Take the call!"

Josh hung up on the president and jabbed Accept.

"Hey!" Lydia said.

"Hey," Josh replied, in as casual a voice as he could muster. "What's up?"

"Well, my roommate's not picking up her phone. So I was thinking, maybe we could grab brunch after all?"

Josh smiled.

"I'd love to."

He gave her directions to his favorite diner, threw on his jeans, and headed out to meet her. A storm of flashbulbs greeted him as he opened his door.

"Josh!"

"Over here! Josh!"

His hallway was clogged with journalists, snapping his picture and shoving microphones into his face. He smiled for the cameras but didn't stop for any interviews. He didn't want to keep Lydia waiting.

After weaving his way through the crowd, Josh finally arrived at the Clark Street Diner. Lydia was standing right outside, chatting on her cell phone. She waved at him happily and finished up her phone call.

"Cool, I'll see you in Paris. Listen, I gotta run. 'Bye!"

She put away her phone and kissed Josh on the cheek. He laughed and kissed her back.

"Who was that?" he asked.

"Oh, some ad firm," she said. "They want me to be the new face of Dior."

"That's cool," Josh said. "Do you like omelets?"

She nodded enthusiastically.

"I *love* them."

"Well, this place makes great ones."

She blushed as he held open the door for her.

"After you," he said.

They entered to the sound of deafening applause.

I Love Girl

I am Oog. I love Girl. Girl loves Boog.

It is bad situation.

Boog and I are very different people. For example, we have different jobs.

My job is Rock Thrower. I will explain what that is. There are many rocks all over the place and people are always tripping over them. So when I became a man at age eleven, the Old Person said to me: "Get rid of all the rocks." Since that day, I have worked very hard at this. Whenever it is light outside, I am either gathering rocks, carrying them up the hill, or throwing them off the cliff. In the past ten years, I have cleared many rocks from the ground. People still trip on rocks, but they trip less than before.

Boog's job is Artist. I will explain what that is. When he became a man, the Old Person said to him: "Cut down the trees so we have space to live." But Boog did not want to do this, so now he smears paints on caves. He calls his smears "pictures." Everybody likes to look at them. But the person who likes to look at them most is Girl.

I love Girl. I will explain what that is. When I look at her, I feel sick like I am going to die. I have never had the Great Disease (obviously, because I am still alive). But my Uncle described it to me. He said there is a tightness in your chest, you cannot breathe, and you have anger toward the Gods because they are hurting you for no reason. I was going to ask him to explain more, but then he died. (He had been sick a long time, almost two days.) My point is: Girl makes me feel this way, like I am going to die. There are many women in the world. By last count, seven. But she is the only one I ever loved.

Girl lives on Black Mountain. It is called Black Mountain because (1) it is mountain and (2) it is covered in black rocks. Every day, Girl has to climb over the rocks to get to the River. It is too hard.

She has small legs and she is often getting stuck. So one day I decided: "I will clear a path from Girl's cave to the River."

I have been working on Girl's path for many years, picking up the black rocks and carrying them away. I never throw her rocks off the cliff like normal rocks. Instead, I put them in a pile next to my cave. I like to look at the pile, because it reminds me of how I am helping Girl. The pile is black and shiny and very big. My mother, who I live with, says it "has to go." She does not understand that it is important to me. (I worry that she will move the pile, but it is unlikely. After all, she is an elderly, thirty-two-year-old woman.)

I have made good progress on Girl's path, but there are still many rocks left to clear. The job would go faster, but I am building the path in secret by the light of the moon. The reason is—and this is a hard thing to admit—I am afraid to talk to Girl. If she found out it was me clearing all the rocks, I'm sure she would say something to me like "Hello" or "Hi there." And then I would be in trouble. Because the truth is: I am not so good at making words.

Boog is very good at making words. For example, last week he showed off his new picture at the Main Cave. Everyone was expecting it to be a horse or a bear (all his pictures so far have been horses, bears, or a mix of horses and bears). But this picture was not of any animal. It was just a bunch of red streaks. People were angry.

"I wanted animals," the Old Person said. "Where are the animals?"

It was a bad situation. I thought that Boog would lose his job or maybe be killed by stones. But then Boog stood on a rock and spoke.

"My art is smart," he said. "And anyone who does not get it is stupid."

Everyone was quiet. We looked at the Old Person to see what he would say.

The Old Person squinted at the red streaks for a while. Then he rubbed his chin and said, "Oh, yes, now I get it. It is smart. People who do not get it are stupid."

A few seconds later, everyone else got it.

"It is smart," they said. "It is smart!"

The only person who did not get it was me. My beard began to sweat. I was scared, you understand, that someone would ask me to make words about the picture.

I headed slowly for the exit. And I was almost out of the cave when Boog pointed his finger at me.

"Do you like it, Oog?"

Everyone stopped making words and looked at me.

"It is smart," I said. I meant for my voice to sound big but it came out small.

Boog smiled.

"Ah," he said. "Then why don't you explain it to us?"

I felt a burning on my skin. It was sort of like when you fall into a fire and your body catches on fire. I looked down at my feet and people started laughing at me.

I looked up at Girl to see if she was one of the ones laughing. She was not (thank Gods). But she could hear all the other people laughing and that was just as bad.

"I am tired from talking to people who are less smart," Boog said. "I am going to mate with Girl now."

He took Girl's hand and started to mate with her. Some people stayed to watch, but most took this as their cue to leave.

On my way out, I heard Girl making sounds. They stayed in my head all night, like an echo in a giant, empty cave.

The next day I decided to become an Artist. I told my plan to Oog (there are several of us named Oog, I am sorry if it is confusing) and he said, "You can't be an Artist. It is hard."

Oog agreed with him.

"You're just a Rock Thrower," he said. "Stick with that."

I was angry at Oog. Partly because he always takes Oog's side. But mostly because I did not agree with his words.

Maybe Artist is hard job. It is not for me to say. But I would be surprised if it was as hard a job as Rock Thrower.

Throwing rocks is not so easy. For example, five years

ago, one of my shoulders detached from my arm when I was throwing a boulder off a cliff. And two years after that, the other shoulder detached also. I can still throw rocks. But now, when I throw them, I am screaming. Not just once in a while, but constantly. Every time I throw a rock I am screaming, so loud. I do not always realize I am screaming—it is just part of my life. Usually, by sundown, I have no voice left. It is gone, you understand, because I was screaming so much from the pain of throwing rocks. Another thing is that sometimes I fall off the cliff, which is a bad situation.

"I am going to make a picture," I told the others. "A good one."

"Who are you going to show it to?" Oog said. "Your mother?"

Everyone laughed: Oog, Oog, Moog, even Oog.

"No," I said. "I will show it to Girl."

No one made words after that.

I have never spoken to Girl, but one time she spoke to me. It was a long time ago, when we were still children.

It was the first day of school and we were learning to count. It was confusing. I am very good at some numbers. I understand "one" and "two" very well and I am okay with "three." But when it gets to higher math, "four," "five," and so on, I get confused.

The Old Person had told us to each make a pile of five rocks. I did not know how many to do and it was getting to be my turn. It was a bad situation.

The Old Person was about to call on me when Girl whispered into my ear.

"You have too many rocks," she said. "You need to take away four."

I stared at her. I think she could tell from my eyes that I did not have a great grasp of "four."

"It's two twos," she said.

I swallowed. To this day I do not know what she meant by this.

"Don't worry," she said. "I will help you."

The Old Person was about to look at my pile when Girl stood up and pointed into the forest.

"Predator!"

By the time we came back from the Hiding Cave, it was nightfall. On the second day of school we graduated and I got my sheepskin just like everybody else. I wanted to thank Girl, but I did not know which words to make. So I said nothing.

Girl has a small head, so it is very strange how she fits so many things inside of it. She knows all of the numbers: "six," "eight"—you name it. But she also knows other things; things nobody else knows.

One time I followed her down to the River. She was hunting fish in the normal way, by jabbing a stick in the water. After a long time, she caught a small flat fish. I assumed she would do the normal thing (rip off the head and eat the body) but instead she did the strangest thing that I have ever seen. She put the stick—with the small fish still on it—back into the river. A short time later, she pulled the stick out. A bigger fish was on the stick.

To this day, I do not understand how Girl did this. But I have thought a lot about what I saw, how she used the stick to get the small fish and then the big fish, and I have developed a theory. My theory is: she is a witch who knows magic.

Even though she is probably a witch, I still love her. My mother says that when you love someone, you love them despite their flaws. For example, my father was not so good at hunting after a monster ate his arms. But my mother continued to mate with him, because she loved him.

Girl must really love Boog, because he has many flaws. He never smiles or shares his meat with other people. He is rude to the Old Person and will not rub his feet. And he isn't very "down to earth." For example, one day he stood on the big rock and said, "I am a living God. Everyone should worship me for I am a living God." Maybe he is right. I do not know how all that works. But he doesn't have to say it on the rock.

Boog's worst flaw, though, in my opinion, is that he disrespects Girl. It is very subtle, but if you watch them closely, you can tell. For example, sometimes he orders her to mate with him in front of crowds. I know this is his right (he is man, she is woman). But it is the *way* he orders her to mate that I do not like. He makes his voice big and snaps his fingers. It is like he is talking to a dog. If I owned Girl, I would only command her to mate with me in front of crowds if it seemed like she was in the mood to do that.

Boog has a lot going for him. He is very wealthy (three skins). He is maybe a God (unclear). He styles his hair in the new cool way (wet). He invented Art. But I still cannot understand why Girl is with him. As my father used to say, "There must be other monsters in that cave that we don't know about."

I decided to make my picture of horses because I knew that was a thing. It took a long time, for many reasons: (1) I could only work nights because of rock-throwing job, (2) it was my first time making art, and (Another Reason) my mother was watching over my shoulder the whole time.

I know she was trying to help me, but some of her words made me feel bad. For example, one time she said:

"You are bad at this. You should stop because you are bad. If Girl sees it, she will not like you because the thing you are making is so bad."

I love my mother and will always rub her feet, but sometimes I think she does not know how to help.

Finally, after many days of work, I finished my picture. I was about to add my handprint when I heard a familiar laugh in the distance.

I turned around; Boog was there.

"What a smart picture," he said, clapping his hands. "You are really smart."

I smiled. It was very nice, I thought, for Boog to say nice things about my picture, especially since we are not friends.

"Thank you," I said.

Boog rolled his eyes.

"I was being *sarcastic.*"

A long time passed. I did not know this word, but was afraid to admit so.

"I am glad you like my picture," I said.

Boog cursed the Gods under his breath and paced around for a while.

"The picture is *bad,*" he said. "Okay? It stinks. I do not like it."

I sighed. For the first time, I was beginning to see what he meant.

My plan, as you know, had been to show my picture to Girl. But I started to become worried that she would not like it. The reviews, so far, were not great.

Oog said: "It is the worst picture made yet by a human."

Moog said: "It is proof that you are a dumb person. Because the quality is poor and also the idea is bad."

The Old Person said: "I always knew you were dumb. It is known by everyone. But this picture makes me realize you are even dumber than it was believed. You are like a beast from the woods, or a rock on the ground. No brain."

One of the main problems, people explained, was that I had not made the right number of legs for the horse. Also, I had made the body too big, so there wasn't enough space for a head. Also, I had given it hands, forgetting that a horse does not have any hands.

I was proud of the picture when I made it; but people's words had made me ashamed. I decided it was best to destroy it before Girl found out about it.

I grabbed some empty bladders and brought up water from the River. I was about to splash the painting when I heard that laugh again.

"Don't destroy it yet," Boog said. "There is someone who wants to see it."

He grabbed Girl by the arm and thrust her in front of my picture. It was a bad situation.

"Tell Oog what you think of it," Boog said.

Girl mumbled something, but it was too soft for me to hear.

"Tell him!" Boog ordered.

"I do not like it," Girl said. "You are not smart. I love Boog and not you."

I stood there in silence. Hot water came out of my eyeballs.

Boog grabbed one of my bladders, wet his hand, and slicked back his hair in his style. Then he walked over to my pile of black rocks, picked one up, and hurled it against my picture.

"Let's go," he said to Girl.

She started to follow him. As she was leaving, though, she paused to take a rock from my pile. I was afraid she would throw it at my picture, like Boog had. But instead she held it up to her face and squinted at it.

"Let's go!" Boog shouted.

She followed him into the woods, still holding the rock in her hand.

My mother woke me in the night.

"A monster is here to murder us," she said.

I nodded. This is usual occurrence.

"What kind of monster? Wolf?"

She shook her head.

"It is a clever monster. Listen."

We were silent for a while; soon, I heard a strange sound. The monster was throwing rocks against the cave, one after the other.

I took my kill stick and headed cautiously for the door. I saw a figure in the shadows and was about to charge it when the moon appeared suddenly between clouds.

"Girl?"

She was standing on the edge of the forest, a black rock in her hand.

"Sorry if I scared you," she said. "I just came to say thank you."

I was confused.

"For what?"

"For building me a path."

"How did you know it was me?"

"I took a rock from your pile and compared it to the ones on my mountain. They're the same kind."

I walked cautiously toward her.

"Are you a witch?" I asked.

She laughed.

"I'm not a witch! I just used common sense. I mean, there are thousands of black rocks piled up next to your cave and they're identical to the rocks that were cleared away from my mountain. It doesn't take a witch to figure out what happened."

I looked her in the eyes.

"If you are a witch," I said, "you can tell me. I will guard your secret."

She put her hand on my arm. All the hairs on it stood up.

"Thank you for clearing all the rocks," she said, looking into my eyes. "It is a good path. You are good at clearing the rocks."

For the second time that night, hot water came out of my eyeballs. Only this time it was because I was happy.

"I'm sorry I said those mean things about your picture," Girl said. "Boog said I had to."

I was shocked; that had not occurred to me. Boog was very clever.

"Does that mean you like my art?" I asked.

She looked at my horse and hesitated.

"It's interesting," she said. "But you know what I really like? Your rock pile."

She walked over to it.

"It's sort of like a sculpture."

"What is sculpture?"

"Like a picture in three dimensions."

Much time passed in silence.

"Can I impregnate you?" I asked.

"What?"

"I know I am not smart like Boog. I do not understand the art and I am bad with the numbers. But I will work hard to clear the rocks for you. And when you have child, I will clear the rocks for the child. I will clear all the rocks for you and the child until I am eaten by a monster or die of the Great Disease. I will make you many paths so you can go all the places you want."

I paused to catch my breath. It was the most words I had ever made at one time.

"What about Boog?" she whispered.

I thought about it for a moment.

"I will murder him," I said. "With a rock."

She smiled and kissed me on the cheek. It was like it had been in my dreams.

We made many words that night. Girl explained that she never really loved Boog. He just seemed like her "only option." He was the only one who had ever asked to mate with her. The other five men on earth had been too afraid, including me.

I confessed to her that I did not understand Boog's latest picture and she laughed.

"No one did," she said. "Not even Boog."

The stars were out and Girl counted them aloud until I fell asleep.

The next day I took a large rock and struck it into Boog's head so that his skull cracked open and he died. Afterward, Girl and I went swimming.

We have decided to have many children: one, two—maybe even a higher number.

I love Girl. Girl loves me.

It is good situation.

BOY GETS GIRL

Scared Straight

KYLE STRUTTED COCKILY THROUGH the yard, his face a mask of indifference.

"Move!" one of the guards shouted at him. "Move, move, move!"

The boy stifled a smirk. He felt sorry for the guards. They'd been screaming at him since sunrise, trying in vain to "break" him. Now it was nearly sundown and their voices were beginning to go hoarse.

Kyle understood why they had put him in the program. Scared Straight was designed for "high-risk youths"—and he clearly fit the bill. Since the Winter Formal, he'd been hooking up with the same girl, Alison, every weekend. And recently, over Gchat, she'd asked him what they were. Still, that didn't mean he'd end up imprisoned in a long-term relationship. He was only seventeen, after all. His entire life lay ahead of him.

He glanced at the other teenagers in his group. They'd all acted tough on the bus ride to Park Slope. But all of them had ended up breaking. Christian had lost it first, during the tour of Belle Cochon.

"Look at this fucking restaurant!" a red-faced guard had screamed at him as he shuffled through the candlelit bistro. "This is the kind of place you're going to have to take her to every Saturday night! Because when you're in a relationship, Saturday night is date night!"

Christian tried to keep it together, but when the guard shoved a menu into his hand and made him read out the price of the steak au poivre, his lips began to quiver.

The other kids managed to hide their fear—until the tour of Bed Bath & Beyond.

"Look at this fucking bench!" a guard shouted at them. "This is the bench you're going to have to fucking sit on while your girlfriend picks out weird shit for the bathroom! And then, when she comes over with two fucking identical light fixtures, you're going to have to pretend you prefer one of them over the other! 'Cause otherwise, she'll say you're not 'participating'! What do you think about that shit?"

By the time they left the store, every kid was trembling.

Every kid except for Kyle. He wasn't scared at all. At worst, he was bored. And now the day was almost over. He just had to get through one more hour of bullshit and he'd be home free.

"Okay, listen up!" a guard shouted. "Your program is coming to a close. But before we let you back onto the street, we've got a speaker for you. His name is Dan Greenbaum. And he's been in a long-term relationship with his girlfriend, Sarah, for *seven years*."

For the first time all day, Kyle felt his shoulders tensing up. He'd never actually met a real inmate before.

The guard took a key out of his pocket and let the prisoner out of his brownstone. He was wearing a standard-issue uniform: khaki pants, Kenneth Cole loafers, and a sweater from Brooks Brothers.

"My name is Dan," he said. "I'm twenty-nine years old. And I'm serving a life sentence as boyfriend to my girlfriend, Sarah."

He paced down the row of teenage boys, his jaw clenched tight with bitterness.

"My story started out simple," he said. "A random hookup, a couple of dates. The next thing I knew, I had a drawer for her clothes in my apartment. Then one day, I looked up, and I was here. Trapped in a Park Slope brownstone for the rest of my goddamn life."

The prisoner stopped pacing—right in front of Kyle.

"What did this punk do?" he asked, staring icily into the teenager's eyes.

The guard checked his clipboard.

"Hooked up with a girl named Alison six times," he read. "She recently asked him 'what they were.' "

The prisoner whistled.

"That's how it starts," he said. "That's how it fucking starts."

He grinned at Kyle.

"You ever hang out with her friends?"

Kyle shook his head awkwardly.

"Why not?" the prisoner asked. "Answer me, boy!"

Kyle swallowed.

"I guess . . . I don't really *like* her friends."

The inmate laughed and clapped his hands sarcastically.

"I don't like my girlfriend's friends, either," he said. "But guess what? I hang out with them every fucking Sunday. Sarah throws a weekly dinner party and invites every one of them over. They quote *Borat* for hours and I have to laugh, like it's a new thing. If I don't, Sarah accuses me of being 'anti-social.' That's my fucking life now! Every single Sunday! A dinner party with her fucking friends who still quote *Borat*! What do you think about that?"

Kyle tried to look away, but the prisoner grabbed him by the chin and pulled his face toward him. Kyle could feel the man's hot breath on his skin.

"You ever hear of Junot Díaz?" he spat.

"No, sir," Kyle mumbled.

"He's a writer," the inmate said. "Sarah's got me reading this book he wrote. It's so fucking boring I can't get past page fifty. My eyes just glaze over. But guess what? I've gotta finish the whole fucking thing, because she signed us up for a book club and I'm going to have to fucking talk about the book in front of her fucking goddamn friends. What do you think about that shit?"

Kyle felt the blood draining from his face. He hoped the prisoner would move on to somebody else. But the inmate could obviously sense that he was on the verge of breaking.

"Want to see some fucked-up shit?" the inmate said, rolling up the sleeve of his sweater. "Check out these fucking triceps. Look how fucking developed they are. That's from Pilates. Do you know what the fuck Pilates is? Neither did I, until I had a long-term girlfriend. Now I've gotta do it every fucking Wednesday because she cried one time and said I needed to get serious about my health! Are you listening to the fucking shit I'm saying?"

Kyle bit his lip, trying his best to keep from crying. The inmate folded his arms and stared off into the distance.

"I used to dream about busting out of here," he said. "Just dumping Sarah and being single again. But now? This life is all I know. I'm an institutional man, pure and simple. Hell, even if she released me, I wouldn't know how to live on the outside. Where would I go to pick up girls? Is Radio Bar still cool? Or is it played out? I don't even know, like, what the cool places are anymore."

He took a step toward Kyle, boring into him with his dark-brown eyes.

"Prison does things to you," he whispered. "Strange things. At first, the routine makes you crazy. But after a few years, you get used to it. Then, at some point, you start to crave it. You start to look forward to the monthly grocery trip to Costco. A new episode of *Mad Men* is enough to get you through a Sunday. Your world's so small you can fit it on the head of a pin. And the sick truth is you *like* it that way."

Kyle felt a scalding tear roll down his cheek. The inmate smiled subtly at the guards; they smiled back at him, nodding with respect.

"Well, I'd love to stay and chat," the inmate told the boys. "But I've gotta go back inside and pack. Sarah just sentenced me to three days in the hole."

Kyle knew he wasn't supposed to ask any questions, but he couldn't help himself.

"What's the hole?" he murmured.

"The hole is what I call her mother's house in Connecticut," the inmate said. "We go there twice a year. Her sister's going to be there this time and the whole thing's going to be a fucking nightmare."

Kyle watched in silence as the inmate shuffled back into his brownstone. Then he took out his cell phone and broke things off with Alison by text.

Center of the Universe

ON THE FIRST DAY, God created the heavens and the earth.

"Let there be light," He said, and there was light. And God saw that it was good. And there was evening—the first night.

On the second day, God separated the oceans from the sky. "Let there be a horizon," He said. And lo, a horizon appeared and God saw that it was good. And there was evening—the second night.

On the third day, God's girlfriend came over and said He'd been acting distant lately.

"I'm sorry," God said. "Things have been crazy this week at work."

He smiled at her, but she did not smile back. And God saw that it was not good.

"I never see you," she said.

"That's not true," God said. "We went to the movies just last week."

And she said, "Lo. That was last *month*."

And there was evening—a tense night.

On the fourth day, God created stars to divide the light from the darkness. He was nearly finished when He looked at his cell phone and realized that it was almost 9:30 p.m.

"Fuck," He said. "Kate's going to kill me."

He finished the star he was working on and cabbed it back to the apartment.

"Sorry I'm late!" He said.

And lo: she did not even respond.

"Are you hungry?" He asked. "Let there be yogurt!" And there was that weird low-cal yogurt that she liked.

"That's not going to work this time," she said.

"Look," God said. "I know we're going through a hard time right now. But this job is only temporary. As soon as I pay off my student loans, I'm going to switch to something with better hours."

And she said unto Him: "*I* work a full-time job and *I* still make time for you."

And He said unto her: "Yeah, but your job's different."

And lo: He knew immediately that He had made a terrible mistake.

"You think my job's less important than yours?" she said.

"No!" God said. "Of course not! I know how difficult it is to work in retail. I'm totally impressed by what you do!"

"Today I had to talk to fourteen buyers, because it's Fashion Week? And I didn't even have time to eat *lunch*."

"That's so hard," God said. "You work so hard."

"How would you know? You never even ask about my day! You just talk about your work, for hours and hours, like you're the center of the universe!"

"Let there be a backrub," God said.

And He started giving her a backrub.

And she said unto Him, "Can you please take the day off tomorrow?"

And He said unto her, "Don't *you* have to work tomorrow? I thought it was Fashion Week."

"I can call in sick."

And God felt like saying to her, "If your job is so important, how come you can just take days off whenever you feel like it?"

But He knew that was a bad idea. So He said to her, "I'm off Sunday. We can hang out Sunday."

On the fifth day, God created fish and fowl to swim in the sea and fly through the air, each according to their kind. Then, to score some points, He closed the door to his office and called up Kate.

"I'm so happy to hear your voice," she said. "I'm having the hardest day."

"Tell me all about it," God said.

"Caitlin is throwing this party next week for Jenny, but Jenny is, like, being so weird about it that I'm not even sure it's going to happen."

"That's crazy," God said.

And she continued to tell him about her friends, who had all said hurtful things to one another, each according to their kind. And while she was repeating something that Jenny had said to Caitlin, God came up with an idea for creatures that roam the earth. He couldn't get off the phone, though, because Kate was still talking. So He covered the receiver and whispered, "Let there be elephants." And there were elephants, and God saw that they were good.

But lo: she had heard Him create the elephants.

"Oh my God," she said. "You're not even listening to me."

"Kate..."

"It's so obvious! You care more about your stupid planet thing than you do about me!"

God wanted to correct her. It wasn't just a planet he was creating; it was an entire universe. He knew, though, that it would be a bad idea to say something like that right now.

"Kate," He said. "Listen. I'm really sorry, okay?"

But lo: she had already hung up on Him.

On the sixth day, God called in sick and surprised Kate at her store in Chelsea. She was in the back, reading a magazine.

"What are you doing here?" she asked.

"I blew off work," He said. "I want to spend the day with you."

"Really?" she said.

"Really," he said.

And she smiled at Him so brightly that He knew He had made the right decision.

They bought some beers at a bodega and drank them on a bench in Prospect Park. And Kate introduced Him to a game her friend Jenny had taught her, called Would You Rather?

"I don't know if I want to play a game," God said. But she made Him play anyway, and after a few rounds, He saw that it was good. They played all afternoon, laughing at each other's responses. When it got cold, God rubbed her shoulders and she kissed Him on the neck.

"You know what I kind of want to do right now?" Kate said.

God tensed up.

"What?"

"See a movie," she said.

And God laughed, because it was exactly what He wanted to do.

They decided to see *The Muppets* because they had heard that it was good. They had a great time and when it was over, God paid for a cab so they wouldn't have to wait all night for the L train.

"I love you," Kate said as she nodded off in the backseat. "I love you so much."

"I love you, too," God said.

And both of them saw that it was good.

On the seventh day, God quit his job. He never finished the earth.

Girlfriend Repair Shop

MAX? *Max.*"

Max swiveled his head toward Dr. Motley.

"Yes?"

"Your girlfriend was just making a very interesting point. About you not listening to her. Were you . . . listening?"

Max sighed.

"I'm sorry," he admitted, his puffy cheeks flushing with embarrassment. "I must've zoned out."

"Unbelievable," Karen said. "Even here, during *this,* he's so self-involved he can't even pay attention to me for five minutes!"

Dr. Motley squinted at Max through his horn-rimmed glasses.

"Do you think there's any truth to what she's saying?"

Max nodded glumly.

"I guess."

Out of the corner of his eye he saw Karen break into a gloating grin. It occurred to him that it was the first time he'd seen her smile in months.

"Have you always had this problem?" Dr. Motley asked. "This tendency to 'zone out'?"

Max hesitated, unsure of how to respond. He'd been zoning out since childhood. But it wasn't until he started dating Karen that his zoning out had been classified as a problem. He was a software designer, and zoning out had led to his best work. He'd perfected algorithms by zoning out, virus-proofed systems by zoning out. Zoning out had paid for the house he shared with Karen and their ten-day trip to Hawaii and the therapy session they were sitting in right now.

"Max?"

Max swallowed and looked up. Dr. Motley and Karen were exchanging a knowing glance.

"I was asking," Dr. Motley said, a slight edge to his voice, "if there are any problems *you* would like to address."

Max let loose a long, defeated sigh. In his mind, there was only one problem with their relationship: two years into it, for no discernible reason, Karen had started being mean to him. It was like a switch had turned in her brain. One day, she was complimenting his beard and mixing him scotch and sodas and asking him about his work. The next day, she was rolling her eyes at his jokes and shrinking away whenever he tried to kiss her. When he asked what was wrong, she became offended. The problem, she insisted, was his: he just didn't know how to make her "feel loved."

"Tell me this," Dr. Motley pressed. "Why did you agree to come here?"

Max looked down at his lap. The truth was, secretly, he had come to be proven right. He'd assumed that a third-party witness (particularly a male one) would take one look at the facts and declare him innocent. His girlfriend would be diagnosed with some mental problem: depression, possibly, or something menstruation-related. She'd be given pills of some kind. And then everything would go back to the way it was, in the beginning, before she went crazy.

"If this relationship is going to work," Dr. Motley was saying, "you're going to have to start paying attention to her needs. She's been feeling vulnerable for months and you've done nothing to validate her."

"I've been trying," Max insisted. "But whenever I ask what's wrong with her—"

"Nothing's wrong with her," Dr. Motley interrupted. "That's what you need to understand. Your girlfriend doesn't need 'fixing.' She just needs you to *listen.* And it's going to take some major effort, on your part, to learn how."

He glanced at the clock.

"We have a little over twenty minutes left. Karen, if it's

all right with you, I'd like to spend some one-on-one time with Max. I think he'd benefit from some individualized treatment."

"I understand," Karen said.

Max could detect a slight bounce in her step as she made her way out of the office. He closed his eyes as the heavy door shut, sealing him in.

"Scotch?"

Max opened his eyes and coughed. To his great surprise, his therapist was pouring out two drinks.

"I don't know," Max said suspiciously.

"Come on," Dr. Motley said. "Don't be a pussy."

Max took a drink and watched in stunned silence as his therapist downed the other.

"Man," Dr. Motley said. "That girlfriend of yours is *nuts*."

Max remained perfectly still, unsure of how to respond. Was this some kind of psychological test?

"Jesus," the doctor said. "You can calm down, okay? I'm on your side."

Max squinted at him.

"You are?"

"Of course I am! You didn't actually buy any of that crap I said, did you?"

Relief slowly seeped through Max's veins and he broke into a childish laugh.

"No!" he said. "Not a word of it!"

He took a swig of scotch and the doctor topped him off.

"Drink up," he said. "This session's costing you a fortune, the least you can do is get a buzz."

Max took another gulp and felt his muscles start to relax. It was only eleven in the morning and he was already fairly drunk. He closed his eyes, letting his body sink pleasurably into his leather armchair.

"I don't get it, though," he said. "Why'd you say she was right about everything?"

The doctor let out a hoarse laugh.

"To get her to leave the room!"

Max laughed along with him.

"So what am I supposed to do?" Max asked. "Just break up with her?"

"That's what I would do," Dr. Motley said. "But I'm not big into girlfriends. I've been a 'whores' guy since college. No fuss, no muss, you know?"

Max finished his drink and sighed.

"The thing is," he said, "I don't want to lose her. I mean, I know things have been hard lately . . . but I still love her."

Dr. Motley took a business card out of his pocket.

"In that case," he said, "there's only one solution."

Max took the card and squinted at the text.

Girlfriend Repair Shop
35 W 45th Street
Open Late

"Ask for Han," Dr. Motley said. "He knows his stuff."

Max stared into the doctor's eyes.

"Is this a joke?"

The therapist laughed.

"No, it's not a joke."

He gestured grandly at his office.

"*This* is."

"I'm so glad we met with him," Karen said. "Now you can finally start working on your issues."

"Yeah," Max said, squinting at a nearby street sign.

46TH STREET. They were almost there.

"Where are we going?" Karen asked.

"I just have to run an errand."

"Right now?"

"It'll only take a second. There—there it is!"

He pointed excitedly at a small dark shop adorned with a fluorescent sign.

"What's GRS?" Karen asked.

"It's, uh... General Radio Supplier. I need to get some new transistors for a project."

Karen rolled her eyes.

"I'll wait outside."

Max swallowed anxiously.

"It might be a while," he said. "Why don't you come in with me? It's so cold out."

Karen sighed and followed Max into the store.

The interior was small and bare: just a table, two chairs, and a cash register.

"What is this place?" Karen asked, folding her arms suspiciously. Max could feel his underarms prickling with perspiration. After a few tense seconds, a short Asian man walked out from behind a red curtain.

"Ah," he said. "You Max?"

Max nodded and Han politely shook his hand, completely ignoring Karen.

"I am Han Woo," he said. "Repairman. Dr. Motley send you, right?"

"What the hell is going on?" Karen asked. "What is this place?"

With zero hesitation, Han jabbed his index finger into Karen's left eyeball.

"Oh my God!" Max screamed. "What the fuck?"

"Is fine, is fine," Han assured him. "See?"

Max looked at Karen. She was frozen, as stiff as a mannequin.

"What did you do?" he asked, his voice shrill with panic. "What did you do to my girlfriend?"

"Just freeze her," Han replied calmly. "See?"

He waved his hand in front of Karen's eyes. Max noticed that her pupils remained rigidly centered.

"How did you . . . ?"

Han ignored him and took a screwdriver out of his pocket. Max watched with horror as Han gently pressed the tip to Karen's forehead, applying pressure to a small mole near her hairline. There was a cranking noise, like when you shift gears on a bicycle, and then Karen's scalp popped open.

Max screamed, but his terror quickly turned to fascination. There was no blood, no brains, no gore—just a grid of wires and microchips. It reminded him of a standard PC motherboard.

"Here is problem," Han said, gesturing at a cluster of transistors. "Is loose, see?"

Max peered anxiously into his girlfriend's head. There did, indeed, appear to be some faulty wiring.

"Has she been acting mean?" Han asked.

Max nodded in amazement.

"How did you know?"

"She probably say, 'I no feel loved,' or something like that."

"Yes! She said that exact thing!"

"Don't worry," Han said. "I fix."

Max watched in awe as the repairman went to work, replacing wires, flipping circuits, tightening bolts. At one point, he wrenched a screw clockwise—and Karen's lips simultaneously curled into a smile. After about an hour, he was finished. He put away his tools, shut Karen's scalp, and walked calmly to the cash register.

"Forty thousand dollars," he said.

Max turned pale.

"What?"

"Forty thousand," Han repeated. "Plus five thousand for Dr. Motley's referral fee."

"I don't know if I can afford that," Max murmured.

"Trust me," Han said. "Worth it."

Max nodded glumly and handed over his MasterCard. As soon as it went through, Han handed Max his receipt and then jabbed his finger back into Karen's eyeball.

Max held his breath as his girlfriend's pupils gradually refocused.

"Sweetie?" he whispered. "Are you okay?"

She kissed him warmly on the cheek.

"I'm great, sugar," she said. "Did you get what you were looking for?"

"Yeah," Max said. "I think so."

She took his hand and led him outside into the sunlight.

"You know," she said, "I don't think that therapist knows what he's talking about."

Max's eyes widened.

"You don't?"

"Nah. I've been so mean to you lately, for no reason. You don't deserve it. Let's just go back to the way things were."

Max started to respond and realized that he was crying.

"I love you so much!" he said.

She laughed and kissed him playfully on the nose.

"I love you, too!" she said.

From then on, things were perfect.

The Adventure of the Spotted Tie

IT WAS A COLD WINTRY EVENING when I last called upon my friend Mr. Sherlock Holmes. I found the great detective in his usual pose, hunched over his writing desk, a smoldering pipe in hand. He glanced at me coolly.

"I see you haven't had much luck at the dog track," he said.

I gasped, for I had indeed just lost the sum of four pounds at the Wimbledon Greyhound Stadium.

"How did you guess?" I asked incredulously.

"I guessed nothing," Holmes replied. "All my conclusions were drawn from simple inference."

He pointed to a bright-green stain on my pant leg.

"That stain could only have been produced from pickled relish," he said. "And that condiment is only served with frankfurters. It is obvious, therefore, that you recently partook of that particular dish."

"That follows logically," I agreed. "But how did you know that I ate my frankfurters at a dog track, of all places?"

"What other conclusion could I have drawn, given the location of the relish stain? It's on your lower pant leg. You clearly ate your meal while in a standing position. It was stadium fare. And the only stadium open during this season is the dog track."

I shook my head with admiration. Even though I had spent decades chronicling the great man's feats, I was still often awed by his deductive prowess.

"But how," I begged, "did you know that I had *lost money* at the races?"

He rolled his eyes, as if the question was too simple to merit a response.

"Your shoulders are covered in precipitation," he said. "And I can tell by the scuffs on your loafers that you have been walking for some distance. Surely, had you any funds at your disposal, you would have hired a hansom cab to transport you back to London. It therefore stands to reason that the track has, as the expression goes, cleaned you out."

I laughed with delight.

"It always seems so simple when you explain it to me!" I cried.

"Everything is simple," he said, "when you view it through the lens of rational deduction."

I glanced at his desk, which was piled high with papers.

"May I ask why you have sent for me?"

"I will require your assistance," he said, "in solving a most unusual case."

I grinned.

"Does it have anything to do with the prime minister's recent kidnapping?"

"Actually," he said, "it's a personal matter. Something with Alyssa."

"Oh," I said.

Alyssa was Holmes's girlfriend. They had been romantically involved for several months now. I, personally, had never particularly enjoyed the woman's company. She was rather rude to Holmes, I felt. For instance, she only expressed interest in his cases when celebrities, such as the royal family, were involved. And she rarely exhibited any affection toward him unless she was asking him for money. Still, despite Holmes's extraordinary powers of observation, he seemed unable to notice Alyssa's shortcomings. He frequently referred to her as his "angel," a term I thought uncharacteristically figurative for a man of his scientific bent.

"I was looking through her overnight bag," Holmes explained, "and I found this spotted tie in the bottom."

I examined the tie in the glare of Holmes's gas lamp. It was stained with what appeared to be lipstick.

"This tie is not mine," Holmes said. "And yet, for reasons not yet understood, it appeared inside her bag."

I nodded awkwardly.

"Huh," I said. "What do you make of that?"

"I haven't yet solved the conundrum," he confessed.

"Maybe you should ask her?" I suggested. "Where is she now?"

"With her personal trainer, Jeremy," he said. "They meet on Monday, Wednesday, and Friday evenings. For her thumb."

"Her thumb?"

"Yes, she strained her thumb knitting."

I squinted at him.

"Wasn't that, like, two years ago?"

"Yes," he said.

"Isn't that a lot of therapy for a thumb?"

"Well, her thumb is very badly strained," Holmes explained. "Jeremy says her rehabilitation could take years. And the exercises he puts her through are rather strenuous. When she comes home from her sessions, she's always exhausted and dazed. She usually heads straight for the bath and then goes right to bed. Sometimes she sleeps for over twelve hours."

A long time passed in silence. I waited patiently for the detective to arrive at what appeared to me to be an obvious conclusion. But it was as if the gears of his deductive wheels were jammed.

"Perhaps someone is trying to dodge the fabric tariff by

smuggling garments into the British Empire," he said. "And they are sneaking them into Alyssa's bag."

"I'm not sure that follows," I said.

"This isn't the first time I've found male apparel in her bag," he continued. "I've found socks, too. Big ones. Like the kind of socks a big man would wear. A big, athletic man."

"Like a trainer?"

"I wonder if Moriarty is involved," he said, ignoring me. "That dastardly criminal is just the man to perpetrate a smuggling scheme!"

"I don't think this has to do with Moriarty," I said.

"I should hope not," he said. "I would hate to see him ensnare my sweet Alyssa in one of his evil plots. Her life is already hard enough. Why, just last night she found out she has to go away for nine days for a thumb therapy retreat."

"A what?"

"You know," he said. "One of those thumb retreats they have now, for when people have problems with their thumbs."

"I don't think that's a thing," I said.

"Of course it's a thing," he snapped. "Alyssa's going on one."

"Is Jeremy going with her on this trip?"

"Of course," Holmes said. "He's her trainer. It follows logically."

"Where's the retreat?"

"Aruba."

"Why there?"

"It follows logically," he said again.

He reached for a syringe and injected himself with liquid cocaine.

"Whoa," I said. I could tell from the serum's viscosity that it was stronger than his customary "7 percent solution."

"What percent was that?" I asked.

The detective ignored me. He had begun to pace rapidly across his flat, his bony hands twitching at his sides.

I was considering telling him some of my inferences about Alyssa when a light knock sounded on the door. It was she. Her brow, I noticed, was damp with perspiration and she had a serene smile on her face.

"Darling!" Holmes cried. "How were your thumb exercises?"

"My what?" she replied.

"Your thumb exercises," he repeated.

"Oh," she said. "Right. They were good. Listen, I need some money for that trip."

"Of course," Holmes said. "It follows."

He reached into his wallet and produced a thick bundle of banknotes.

"It follows," he mumbled, more to himself than anyone else.

I glanced out the window. A broad-shouldered man in athletic gear was standing on the corner of Baker Street, a sly grin on his face.

Alyssa pocketed the money, blew Holmes a kiss, and then ran down the stairs. Through the window I saw her skip across the street and into the muscled arms of her lover.

Holmes was back at his desk, the spotted tie in his hand.

"Maybe it was Moriarty," he said, again.

I took a seat beside my friend and patted him gently on the back.

"Maybe," I said.

Celebrity Sexceptions

My friend Jenny taught me a fun game," Kim said. "It's called Celebrity Sexceptions."

Chris rolled his eyes.

"Come on," Kim said, tugging his sleeve. "I promise, it's a fun one."

"Okay, okay. How does it work?"

"We each write down the names of three celebrities," she said. "And if we ever run into them, we get to have an affair with them. They're our sex*ceptions*. Get it?"

Chris chuckled.

"Sounds like a trap."

"It's not!"

"Really?" Chris said. "You're not going to get jealous? No matter which actresses I put down?"

"I won't get jealous," Kim said. "I promise."

She playfully thrust out her palm and Chris reluctantly shook it.

"Okay," he said, forcing a smile. "Let's play."

Kim squealed and ran off into the kitchen. She emerged seconds later, holding two pads of paper and an unopened box of ballpoints.

"You really prepared for this," Chris joked.

She took off her watch and rested it on the coffee table.

"You have five minutes," she said in a stern voice. "And then your time is up."

"You're the boss."

He stared down at his pad and sighed. Kim was obviously testing him. She was feeling self-conscious about some physical trait—her breasts or her ass or God knows what. If he put down women who bested her in any one physical category, she'd be furious at him for days. The only way out of the mess was to be as eclectic as possible in his picks. That way his answers would reveal nothing about his tastes.

"Okay," he said, after a couple of minutes of intense concentration. "I'm ready."

She leaned back on the couch and smiled expectantly.

"Christina Hendricks," he said, "Gwyneth Paltrow, and Tina Turner."

Kim raised her eyebrows.

"Tina Turner?"

Chris shrugged.

"She's always done it for me," he said.

"Okay," Kim said cheerfully. "I hereby grant you those sexceptions."

Chris sighed with relief. It hadn't been easy, but he'd managed to pass her exam. He was about to flick on the television when Kim nudged him with her foot.

"Don't you wanna hear mine?" she said.

"Oh, yeah," he said. "Sorry. Go ahead."

She took a deep breath.

"Brad Pitt," she read, "Leonardo DiCaprio . . . and Sam Magdanz."

Chris squinted at her.

"What?"

"Sam Magdanz," she repeated. "Your brother, Sam Magdanz."

"But . . . Sam's not a celebrity."

"He was on *Wheel of Fortune* once."

"That was, like, eight years ago. And he didn't even win. I think he came in third."

There was a long silence.

"Chris," she said. "We need to talk."

Wishes

CLAIRE WAS WALKING UP the stairs to her apartment when she smelled smoke. She coughed a few times and anxiously quickened her pace. By the time she made it up to her floor, her eyes were burning. The hallway was clogged with purplish fog.

She knocked on her door in a panic.

"Gabe!"

Her boyfriend didn't respond. Claire rummaged through her purse, found her key, and swung the door open. Through the haze, she could make out Gabe's scrawny shape. He was sitting on the couch, holding a strange bronze vessel in his hand.

"Honey!" he called out. "Wow—you're home early."

"Why is it so smoky in here?" she asked. "What's that thing you're holding?"

Gabe hesitated.

"It's a genie lamp."

"What?"

"I'm serious," he said. "Look, I'll show you."

He rubbed the lamp and smoke poured out of its spout. Claire watched as the purple plumes cohered into a giant, muscled creature. He had a bright-red turban, golden chains, and a long black beard.

"State your wish!" the genie roared in a booming baritone. "And the Great Mumbafa shall grant it!"

"Oh my God," Claire said, sitting down beside her boyfriend. "Where'd you get this thing?"

"EBay," Gabe said. "I thought it was just a regular lamp, but then this genie popped out."

"This is amazing!"

"I know, right? We have two wishes and we can use them on whatever we want. World peace, a cure for cancer..."

"Wait, hold on," Claire said. "*Two* wishes? Don't genies give you three?"

"I think it's usually two," Gabe said.

"Really?"

"Yeah," Gabe said. "I'm pretty sure it's two."

A faucet turned on suddenly in the bathroom.

"What's that?" Claire asked. "Is someone else here?"

"Yeah!" Gabe said. "I forgot to tell you. Uh... Marisa Tomei is here."

"Who?"

"Marisa Tomei."

"What's she doing here?"

"Well, her car broke down. Outside our building. So I had her come inside to call Triple A. Because her phone was broken, too, so she needed a phone, so I said, 'Hey, we've got a phone, use our phone!'"

Claire turned toward the genie.

"How many wishes did you grant him?"

The genie averted his eyes.

"Great Mumbafa stay out of this," he said.

He tried to funnel back into the lamp, but Claire rubbed the surface, forcing him out again.

"I *wish* for you to tell me," she said.

"You will be down to just one wish."

"I don't care."

The genie sighed.

"Okay," he said. "The number of wishes he originally had... was fifty."

"Fifty?"

She stared at Gabe with contempt.

"You used forty-eight wishes already? Jesus Christ! They were all sex wishes, weren't they?"

Gabe looked down at the carpet.

"What did he wish for?" Claire asked the genie.

"Great Mumbafa don't want to go into it."

"I *wish* for you to tell me."

"You'll be out of wishes."

"I don't care."

The genie sighed again.

"Well, it was all sex things, obviously."

"All with Tomei?"

"The first few were Tomei. But he got bored with that. By the end he was pretty 'all-over-the-place.'"

"I can't believe this!" Claire shouted.

Her eyes welled up with angry tears. Gabe tried to put his hand on her shoulder, but she violently shook him off. A minute passed in silence. Eventually, the genie cleared his throat.

"Can Great Mumbafa say something?"

Neither Claire nor Gabe responded. The genie decided to keep going.

"Great Mumbafa see this all the time," he said. "A woman finds her boyfriend's genie, checks his wish history, and flips out. But trust me, your boyfriend is not a freak or anything. This is just what guys do."

Claire rolled her eyes.

"I am serious," the genie said. "Why do you think there is no world peace? Because no man ever wishes for it. All of them have the option. Sometimes, Great Mumbafa even say, 'How about world peace? You can use one of your many wishes on world peace.' But no man ever takes me up on it. It is always Helen of Troy, or Nefertiti, or, for brief period in nineties, Téa Leoni."

Claire looked up at the genie, her cheeks damp with tears. "Really?"

"Really," the genie said.

Gabe turned toward his girlfriend.

"I'm really sorry," he said. "I'm so embarrassed."

Claire sighed.

"Just get Marisa Tomei out of here."

Gabe marched obediently into the kitchen, grabbed Marisa Tomei by the elbow, and ushered her out the door. Claire couldn't help marveling at the actress's beauty.

"How does she look so *good?*" she asked. "Isn't she, like, in her late forties?"

The genie nodded. "Even Great Mumbafa impressed."

Confidence

JAKE COULD TELL BY THE WAY Meg was chewing her lip that there was something on her mind.

"Is everything okay?" he asked.

"Yeah," she said. "Everything's fine."

She laid her head on his chest.

"It's just... I guess, I've been thinking... what *are* we, exactly?"

Jake winced. Ever since they'd started sleeping together, he'd known this conversation was inevitable.

"Do we really have to *define* things?" he said.

Meg shrugged.

"I just want to know where this is going. We've been doing... whatever it is we're doing... for over two months."

She scratched Jake's scalp and smiled sweetly at him.

"I just want to be your girlfriend," she said softly. "Is that such a crazy thing to ask?"

Jake smiled as she ran her fingers through his hair. He'd resisted commitment for so long. But why? It wasn't like he'd be giving up anything. The truth was, he hadn't slept with anyone but Meg since the day they met. He'd tried—on numerous occasions. It just hadn't worked out. If he committed to a relationship, he'd at least be getting some credit for his monogamy.

He looked up at Meg. She was smiling warmly at him, her eyes wide with hope. He'd never been with anyone so sweet. She was always scratching his back and massaging his neck. This morning, she'd made him huevos rancheros, with extra onions, just the way he liked them. She wasn't particularly attractive, but neither was he. He was lucky to have found someone who wanted him, someone who needed him so badly she feared she might lose him.

"Okay," he said. "I'm in."

He smiled at her expectantly, anticipating a giddy reaction. But Meg just stared at him in silence, a blank expression on her face. After a moment, he realized she wasn't breathing.

"Meg?" he shouted. "Meg!"

He waved his hands in front of her face, but she didn't respond. When he spotted the TV, he gasped. He didn't have a DVR, but somehow, the television had paused. His entire room was frozen.

"Greetings, Jake," intoned an odd metallic voice.

He spun around frantically. Standing before him were

three strange women with gleaming red eyes and smooth green flesh. Their faces were angular and their bodies long and lean. They were naked beneath diaphanous robes, which clung to their large, throbbing breasts.

"We are Sex Aliens from the Planet Sex," the middle one said. "We have come to request an orgy."

She snapped her fingers and the three of them flung off their robes. One of the garments landed on Meg's head, partially obscuring her frozen face.

"Whoa!" Jake said. "Whoa, whoa . . . whoa."

The middle alien raised her twiglike eyebrows.

"What is wrong?"

"I—I'm sorry," Jake stammered. "But . . . I can't do this."

He covered his face with his hands and sighed.

"I'm in an exclusive relationship."

The alien folded her arms beneath her breasts.

"Since when?"

"Like . . . a few seconds ago."

"Huh," the alien said. "That's too bad."

She parted her lips, revealing a row of gleaming white teeth.

"Are you sure you wouldn't like to have sex with us anyway?" she asked. "We have stopped time to allow the cheating to occur without consequences."

"That's very thoughtful," Jake murmured. "But I can't. I'm just... I'm not that kind of guy."

"Aww," the aliens said in unison.

"Can I ask you something?" Jake said. "Why did you pick *me*? I mean, it's not like I'm that good-looking or anything."

"Our eyesight is poor," the middle alien explained. "We see only shapes and shadows. But our noses are extremely well developed."

"So... I smell good?"

"You smell *confident*," she said. "When a man is desperate, he gives off a foul stench, like a rotting egg. A confident man, though, gives off a glorious bouquet—like a finely charred steak rubbed with truffle oil."

Jake smiled proudly.

"Wow," he said. "I've never thought of myself as confident."

"You are," the alien said. "We could smell it all the way from the Sex Galaxy. As soon as we got a whiff of it, we teleported straight over."

Jake's face flushed as she started to walk toward him. Before long, her breasts were pressing against his chest.

"Are you sure?" she asked, licking her lips.

Jake swallowed. He knew he might never get another chance like this one for as long as he lived. But he wasn't the type of guy who cheated on his girlfriend. Only horrible people did that.

Jake clenched his jaw. He was determined to hold his ground.

"I'm sorry," he said, his voice breaking. "But I can't help you."

The aliens twitched their noses in unison. It was clear that they were disappointed.

"Well, here's my number," the nearest alien said, handing him a strip of paper with about a hundred digits on it. "If you change your mind, just give us a call."

The aliens nodded at each other and then vanished, leaving behind a flash of blinding light. Jake covered his eyes in pain. When he removed his hands from his face, Meg was throwing her pudgy arms around his body.

"I'm so happy!" she said.

"About what?"

"That . . . we're a couple."

"Oh, right," Jake said. "Yeah. Me too."

"Oh, man," Mitch said, "I've been *there*."

Jake stared at his friend.

"You *have*?"

Mitch signaled for another round of beers.

"Sex Aliens stopped by my apartment five years ago," he said. "It was right after I started dating Rachel. There were at least a dozen of 'em."

"Jesus," Jake said. "Was it hard to resist?"

Mitch's lips curled into a grin.

"Who said I resisted?"

Jake's eyes widened with shock. Mitch loved Rachel. They were getting married in two months. How could he have *cheated* on her?

"Did she find out?" he asked.

"Did who find out?"

"Rachel."

"Oh, no," Mitch said. "They did that time-stop thingy."

The beers arrived and Jake took a giant swig. He was feeling a little bit light-headed.

"How do you deal with the guilt, though? I mean, you must regret it."

"The only thing I regret," Mitch said, "is not videotaping it."

He leaned in close and continued in a whisper.

"I don't believe in God," he said. "But sometimes, when I'm lying in bed and Rachel's snoring, I pray that the Sex Aliens will return."

He banged the bar with frustration.

"It'll never happen, though. With girls like that? You're lucky if you even get one chance."

"Huevos rancheros!"

Jake forced a smile as Meg plopped the plate onto the table. Somehow, the dish looked less appetizing than he remembered it. He gamely forked a bite into his mouth, but he could barely choke it down. It had a vaguely bitter taste, like it had been made with rotten eggs.

"Everything okay?" Meg asked.

She started to massage his neck, but he shook her off.

"I'll be right back," he mumbled.

He hurried into the bathroom and locked the door. The walls were too thin to risk a phone call, so he tapped out a simple text: "I changed my mind!" He entered the alien's phone number as quickly as he could and pressed the Send button. It took a few minutes, but at last the message went through.

"Are you okay?" Meg called out from the hallway.

"Yeah!" he responded. "Just give me a minute!"

He stared at his phone, but no response came. He reread his text to the aliens and grimaced. The exclamation point had probably been unnecessary.

He sent another message, this one more direct: "Please come over."

Five minutes passed in silence. He could hear Meg pacing nervously on the other side of the door.

"Sure you're okay, honey?" she asked.

"I'm *fine,*" he growled.

He sent another text—then another, and another. But he knew it was hopeless. They were never coming back. He was desperate again—and they could smell it.

The Important Thing

I NEVER ADMITTED IT TO ALAN, but the truth is, I never really liked any of his girlfriends. Nikki, Kendal, Jackie—they all gave me a really bad vibe. They were super-attractive; Kendal, I think, had even been a model. But there was just something so *cold* about them. They were always demanding gifts—jewelry and dresses and extravagant vacations. And if Alan ever did anything to upset them, they'd punish him for days, ignoring his phone calls and making him feel like garbage. I've been best friends with Alan since kindergarten, and I always felt like he deserved better. So when I found out he was dating Mother Teresa, I was thrilled. At last, he'd found somebody sweet and kind and nurturing. Somebody *warm*. It was a real miracle.

I got along with Teresa from the start. She was adorable, obviously, with her blue-and-white sari and her knobby little fingers and her squeaky Albanian accent. And I was inspired, of course, by her decades of devotion to the world's poor. But what impressed me the most about Teresa was how much she loved Alan. In order to enter into a relationship with him, she'd had to make an exception to her holy vows. She was so crazy about him, though, that it hadn't been an issue. From the moment they met, she was at his apartment constantly. And if she ever had to leave town, to start an AIDS hospice or something, she texted him nonstop. When Alan told me they were getting married, I wasn't surprised at all. It was obvious they were made for each other.

As best man, it was my duty to organize the bachelor party. I wasn't sure how wild to make it, so I had lunch with Teresa before planning things. As usual, she was super-cool about everything.

"I know what occurs at such parties," she whispered. "And I am at peace with it."

I ended up renting out the banquet room at Club Lime and booking a stripper named Aja.

The party started at ten, so I got there at nine, to make sure everything was set up properly. To my surprise, Alan was already there. He was sitting alone at the bar, finishing up a martini. I smacked him on the back and laughed.

"Looks like this party's already getting started!"

"Yeah," he said. "Yeah."

I could tell he was a bit nervous—which was completely understandable. He had no idea what sort of night I'd planned. Part of me wanted the stripper to be a surprise, but I didn't want my friend to suffer any longer.

"Don't worry," I said. "I talked to Teresa. She knows I hired a stripper and she's totally cool with it."

"Uh-huh," he said. He didn't seem to be listening to me. He caught the bartender's eye and signaled for another martini.

"Whoa," I said. "Pace yourself. Long night ahead of us."

He gripped my arm suddenly.

"I need to talk to you," he said. His eyes looked bloodshot, like he hadn't slept the night before.

"What's the matter?" I joked. "Cold feet?"

I laughed for a bit—but his expression remained rigid and grave.

"I need to talk to you," he repeated. "In private."

I ordered a martini of my own and followed him into the lap-dance room.

Alan took a swig of gin and grimaced. He isn't much of a drinker, and he was already beginning to slur his words a bit.

"Look," he said. "Teresa's great. She's sweet, she's nice. Honestly, she's like a *saint*."

I squinted at him.

"Then what's the problem?"

He sighed.

"It's so stupid and *small*—I feel like an idiot for even saying it...."

"I'm your best man," I said. "You can tell me anything."

He fiddled with his martini stirrer for a while.

"Teresa's great," he said again. "She's the *best*. It's just..."

He averted his eyes.

"I'm not that attracted to her."

"You mean...?"

Alan nodded.

"Sexually."

"Oh," I said, trying my best to act casual. "Huh. Well... when did that start?"

"Pretty much from the beginning," he admitted. "At first I didn't think much of it. I figured, you know, the relationship's still new, we're still learning each other's bodies. I kept waiting for things to improve. But they never did."

I nodded awkwardly. The truth is, even though we've been best friends for years, we don't usually talk about these sorts of things.

"Listen," I said. "Couples have those sorts of problems all the time. Maybe you just need to be more... adventurous?"

"That's not the problem," he said. "She's *very* adventurous."

"Really?"

"Yeah," he said with a slight shudder. "Anyway, my point is, I'm afraid we're just not sexually compatible."

"Is it her age?" I asked gently.

"That's part of it. I mean, obviously, she's incredibly old. But it's also certain things about her body. I won't go into specifics, but..."

He stared off into the distance for a while.

"I won't go into specifics," he repeated.

"Look," I said. "Weddings are stressful. Me and Julie? We barely *spoke* the week before our wedding. Trust me, things will get better on your honeymoon."

"Maybe."

"Where are you guys going, anyway?"

"Central Africa. She's starting a leper colony."

"Oh."

I heard some laughter in the distance. The gang was starting to show up.

"I'm worried she has it," Alan whispered.

"What?"

"Leprosy," he said. "What if she's got it?"

I shook my head firmly.

"She doesn't have leprosy. I mean—you'd be able to tell."

"Would I?" he snapped. "Her skin's already so messed up from all the years in the desert. What if she's got *leprosy?*"

I heard glasses clinking in the next room and the rumble of a Pearl Jam song. The party was in full swing.

"We should probably get out there," I said.

Alan didn't respond. He had begun to pace back and forth, a look of panic on his face.

"Don't worry," I whispered. "Everything's going to be fine."

"How do you know?" he cried.

"Because you *love* her."

Alan sighed.

"I guess that's the important thing," he said. "Right?"

"It's the *only* thing," I said.

Alan stopped pacing. For the first time all night, something close to a smile appeared on his face.

"She is pretty amazing," he said. "You know, this morning I cut myself shaving and she hobbled right over and applied a salve. By the time I got to work, my face was completely healed."

"That's so cool," I said. "Julie would never do that. She can't even watch *House*—she's afraid she'll see blood!"

Alan chuckled.

"Teresa loves *House*."

He looked me in the eyes and grinned.

"Thanks for talking to me. I'm sorry for being so crazy."

He polished off his drink.

"Besides," he said, "I'm sure it'll get better after we're married. I mean, it's probably just something we have to work on."

"Totally," I said.

"And even if it doesn't get better, who cares? I mean, it's just sex, right?"

"Exactly!" I said. "Who cares?"

A boisterous cheer sounded in the next room.

"Uh-oh," I said. "Looks like Aja has entered the building."

I opened the door a crack and we watched the stripper remove her coat. She slid it off slowly, revealing her smooth, bare shoulders and her high, firm breasts.

Alan stared at her for a moment, his jaw clenched tight.

"Come on," I said, forcing a laugh. "Let's get this over with."

My friend sighed heavily and followed me out into the light.

The Last Girlfriend on Earth

So where's he taking you?" Leon asked, trying to sound as nonchalant as possible.

"I think we're just going to have dinner," Ellie said. "Pretty cool, huh?"

"Yeah," Leon answered robotically. "Cool."

Ellie ran her fingers through his thinning hair and kissed him playfully on the nose.

"Baby?" she asked. "Are you jealous?"

"No," Leon lied.

Ellie laughed.

"He just wants to hear my perspective on the Epidemic. I mean, I have a pretty unique perspective."

"I know!" Leon sputtered. "It totally makes sense that he wants to talk to you. I just..."

He looked down at his lap.

"I just don't understand why it has to be at his *house*."

"Because his house is the *White House*."

Leon tried to turn away, but she grabbed his chin and tilted his face toward hers.

"Sweetie," she said. "If the president makes a pass at me, I'll just tell him the truth. That I have a wonderful boyfriend whom I love more than anything in the world."

Leon sighed. He knew that Ellie would never do anything to hurt him. They'd been through so much together in the past three years. Still, it was hard not to be paranoid when your girlfriend was the last woman on earth.

He threw his lanky arms around her body and squeezed so hard that she started to giggle. He was about to kiss her when she cocked her head suddenly toward the window. Outside, the drone of an engine sounded, as loud as a lion's roar.

"Oh my God!" she gasped. "It's Air Force One!"

She smoothed out her dress.

"How do I look?" she asked, twirling around in a circle.

Leon realized with mild panic that she was wearing her sexiest outfit: a backless black dress. In profile, he could see the sides of her breasts. He wanted to tell her to change, but he knew the request would infuriate her.

"You look beautiful," he mumbled.

Ellie laughed and kissed him on the crown of his balding head. In heels she was slightly taller than him.

"Don't wait up," she said as she headed out the door.

The Epidemic struck in the fall of '13, just a few weeks after they'd moved in together. Leon didn't know about her immunity at first, so he tried to shield her from the virus, feeding her vitamins and draping every window with plastic sheeting. But as the weeks passed, their fear gradually subsided, replaced by a cautious optimism. The government scientists arrived in December, a few days before Christmas, and confirmed all of their hopes. Ellie was perfectly healthy—completely unaffected by the plague.

"So I can go outside?" she asked one scientist, a tall bearded man in a white lab coat.

"You can go anywhere," he told her, smiling broadly. "In fact, I've got Knicks tickets for tomorrow night. Courtside. Perhaps you'd like to join me?"

That was when it had started.

In the months since, Ellie had received over ten thousand marriage proposals from billionaires, movie stars, generals, athletes, and kings. Love letters arrived each day—a bushel of envelopes heaved into their entryway by a squat Cuban mailman who always seemed to linger a second too long. When Leon and Ellie went outside, the blitz intensified. So many drinks got sent to her at restaurants that they often ran out of table space. When she hailed a cab, men had fistfights in the street for the chance to open the door for her.

And then there were the assault attempts. Nobody had been successful so far—thank God. But Ellie had used her Taser too many times to count. When Leon first bought her the weapon, she laughed out loud and accused him of being ridiculous. She wouldn't even hold the thing at first—he'd had to place it in her bag for her. Now she was so proficient with the device she could hit a man's neck from twenty yards away, sometimes while maintaining a conversation.

Leon often wished he could keep Ellie locked in their apartment so nobody could hoot at her, or grab her ass, or worse. But he knew that wasn't fair. She was a strong, confident woman and he had no right to try to control her. All he could do was trust her and love her and hope for the best.

"What's wrong, love?" Leon asked when she slunk into bed at 4 a.m.

"Nothing," she murmured.

"Sweetie, if something happened, you can tell me."

Ellie sighed.

"He tried to kiss me," she said, her jaw clenched with rage. "What gives him the right? Sure, he's the president. Sure, he has a secret safety orb. So fucking what?"

Leon squinted at her.

"He's got *what* kind of orb?"

She rolled her eyes.

"Under the earth's crust. He's got some kind of massive bunker built. It's ten square miles, with a self-sustaining forest, and a thousand years of rations, blah, blah, blah. He asked me to go down there with him and his scientists. He wants to nuke civilization and start a 'new world order' with me as his mate."

"I told you so," Leon muttered.

Ellie glared at him and he averted his eyes, instantly regretting his comment.

"What?" she snapped. "*What* did you say?"

Leon swallowed.

"You know," he said. "I just meant that... I told you that sort of thing might happen."

"Not every guy is trying to fuck me, okay? Some men—and this might shock you—are actually interested in me as a *human being.*"

Leon winced. They'd had so many versions of this argument. There was the time Bill Gates asked her to "advise him on philanthropy." Or the time Bono asked her to "cosponsor a fund-raiser." There was the time Mario Batali wanted her to sample a "five- course meal" or the time Cornel West asked her to "guest star on a spoken-word album." All of these invitations had led to sexual advances. West, she'd had to Tase. Still, whenever Leon warned her that a man might have ulterior motives, she exploded with indignation.

"I bet you think Brad's trying to sleep with me," she said.

Leon sighed. He did indeed think that.

"I just find it a little interesting that Brad Pitt—who lives in *California*—would hire a Brooklyn-based interior designer to decorate his beach house. It's not that you're not talented—you're great at what you do. I just think it's pretty *strange* that he didn't hire somebody local."

She turned away from him and flicked out her light.

"Sweetie," Leon whispered in the dark. "I'm sorry."

"Good night."

"Sweetie, don't do this."

He tried to rub her shoulder, but she shook him off. There was nothing he could do but retreat to his side of the bed.

He thought back to the early months of their relationship, a heady blur of laughter, wine, and sex. Sometimes, she would text him in the middle of the afternoon, begging him to leave the office early.

"Please," she'd write. *"I need you."*

He'd find her in the bedroom, already under the sheets, her nude arms reaching out to grasp him.

Now he was always the one who begged for it; and nine

times out of ten she turned him down. Part of the problem was exhaustion. (Ellie had to go to the military lab five days a week so the scientists could do studies on her body, and by the time she got home, all she wanted was a bath.) But Leon knew he couldn't blame fatigue for everything.

He looked at Ellie. Her eyes were clamped shut, her little hands balled up beneath her chin.

"I love you," he whispered.

She didn't respond. He stared at her for a minute, wondering if she was actually asleep.

Kayla was a senior at the New Brunswick Girls' Reformatory when the Epidemic struck. Since there weren't any males at her school, she assumed that the plague had affected both sexes equally. She spent two years alone on her isolated campus, convinced she was the last person alive. It was boredom more than anything that spurred her to steal a car and drive off toward civilization.

"I just don't get what people see in her," Ellie said, flipping through the latest issue of *Vanity Fair.* "She's not even really that pretty."

Leon peeked over her shoulder. Like every magazine on earth, *Vanity Fair* had run a cover story on Kayla. She was wearing a prison uniform in the pictures, her orange jumpsuit partially unzipped to reveal her youthful cleavage.

"I think she's kind of interesting," Leon admitted. "I mean, two years ago she was arrested for stealing lingerie. Now she's dating Bill Clinton."

"She's dating Bill Clinton?"

"You didn't know that?"

He passed her the new issue of *People;* the couple was posing happily on the cover.

"I'm sure the scientists will want to do tests on her," Leon said. "Wouldn't it be cool if we ran into her at the lab?"

"Yeah," Ellie answered robotically. "Cool."

"I love your hair!" Kayla said to Ellie, running her fingers through it. "It's, like, you're not even trying."

"Thanks," Ellie muttered.

"It's so nice to hang out with a girl again! I mean, I guess you're more of a woman. How old are you? Thirty-five?"

"Thirty-one."

"Oh."

Leon cleared his throat.

"So, Kayla," he said. "How are the scientists treating you?"

Kayla rolled her eyes and made a gag gesture.

"If one more scientist asks me out, I'm going to shoot myself."

Ellie nodded.

"I can relate."

"You don't understand," Kayla said. "They're, like, all over me."

There was a long silence. Eventually, Kayla clapped her hands and squealed.

"Hey!" she said. "We should all go out to dinner! Mario Batali wants me to sample a ten-course meal."

Ellie's eyes widened.

"*Ten*-course?"

"That sounds great," Leon said politely. "Maybe you can invite your boyfriend and make it a double date?"

Kayla made another gag gesture.

"I dumped him."

Leon raised his eyebrows.

"You dumped Bill Clinton? Why?"

"He was just so egotistical. I like a guy who's modest, you know? Plus he was too tall. I like men to be closer to my size. You know, like you."

Leon blushed and tilted his eyes toward the floor. When he looked up he noticed that Ellie was glaring at him.

"Thanks for the invite," she said. "But I'm exhausted."

Kayla grinned at Leon.

"Then I guess it's just the two of us!"

Leon fixed his tie in the mirror.

"How do I look?"

"Fine," Ellie said.

He kissed her on the forehead. In socks she was slightly shorter than him.

"Have fun," she mumbled.

"Is something wrong?"

"No."

He smirked.

"Sweetie," he said. "You're not jealous, are you?"

Ellie forced a laugh.

"Of course not!"

They stared at each other for a moment in silence.

Then they took off their clothes and fucked for the first time in weeks.

BOY LOSES GIRL

Is It Just Me?

When I found out my ex-girlfriend was dating Adolf Hitler, I couldn't believe it. I always knew on some level that she'd find another boyfriend. She's smart, cool, incredibly attractive—a girl like that doesn't stay single forever. Still, I have to admit, the news really took me by surprise.

I first found out about them from my friend Paul. We were at Murphy's Pub, watching the World Cup. Argentina was playing, and when they showed a close-up of the crowd, he chuckled.

"I wonder if we'll see Anna and Adolf!"

I could tell by how casually the names rolled off his tongue that they'd been a couple for a while. Everyone, apparently, had been keeping the news from me. I took a sip of bourbon and forced a smile.

"Yeah," I said. "I wonder if we'll see them."

Paul's eyes widened.

"You knew they were dating, right?"

"Of course!" I lied. "I mean, everyone knows *that*."

That night, with some help from Facebook, I pieced it all together. Anna met Hitler a few months after dumping me while vacationing in Buenos Aires. He'd been in hiding there ever since the war, earning money as a German-language tutor. She saw him at a café, recognized his moustache, and struck up a conversation. They hit it off almost immediately.

The relationship progressed quickly, and within a few months, he'd agreed to move into her place in Prospect Heights. It made me nauseous to think about them sharing that apartment. I could still picture it vividly—the clanging of her radiator, the smell of her toothpaste, the softness of her sheets. He'd taken all of it away from me. I knew it was irrational, but I couldn't help hating the guy.

A few weeks later, I was at a friend's party when Anna strolled in with the fuehrer. I bolted for the kitchen and closed the door behind me. I hadn't seen Anna since we broke up. What was I going to say to her? And what was I going to say to Hitler?

"You've got to at least say hi to them," Paul begged me. "If you don't, things will get weird."

"Things are already weird," I said. "She's dating Adolf Hitler!"

Paul stared at me blankly.

"So?"

I closed my eyes and massaged my temples.

"Well, for starters, he's a hundred and twenty-four. That makes him old enough to be her great-great-grandfather."

Paul shrugged.

"Other than the wheelchair, he seems pretty youthful."

I craned my head out the door just in time to hear Hitler quote a line from *Parks and Recreation*. His accent was pretty thick, but Anna burst into laughter anyway. The sound of it made my stomach hurt. We'd dated for almost two years and I couldn't remember ever making her laugh like that.

"I just don't like that guy," I whispered. "I mean, he murdered millions of people."

Paul laughed.

"You don't like him because he's dating Anna."

I sighed.

"Maybe," I admitted. "But don't you think it's weird she's dating him, of all people? I mean, I'm Jewish—he hates Jews..."

"Don't make this about you," Paul said. "Come on, you need to be adult about this."

He grabbed my shoulder and shoved me into the living room. As soon as Anna saw me, she sprinted over and hooked her skinny arms around my torso.

"How are you!" she cooed.

"Great!" I answered, my body tensing. "Really great!"

Hitler wheeled over and stretched out his palm.

"Nice to meet you," he said. "Adolf Hitler."

"Hi," I said, shaking his hand. "Seth Greenberg."

Hitler's pale lips curled into a grin.

"Greenberg?" he said. "Uh-oh!"

Everyone laughed, and I had no choice but to join in. I looked down at my cup; somehow, I was already out of bourbon.

"Seth's an artist," Anna told Hitler. "You should buy some of his paintings."

I started to protest but she ignored me.

"Adolf's got a great collection, but I keep telling him, he needs to get some postwar pieces."

I watched as she ran her fingers across his scalp, delicately massaging his spotted, wrinkled head.

"I used to paint when I was your age," Hitler told me, clearly trying to be polite. "Do you have a website?"

"Come on," Anna urged me. "Tell him."

"It's sethgreenbergpaints.com," I mumbled.

Hitler neatly copied it down in his address book. Then he wheeled to the bar, grabbed a nearly empty bottle of Jim Beam, and poured the last of it into his red plastic cup.

Anna had cut her hair short, but otherwise she looked

better than ever. Her skin was tan from her trips to Argentina, and her smile was wide and bright.

"I miss you," I said, in spite of myself.

She chuckled.

"Seth, you're drunk! Let's get you a glass of water."

She started to walk to the kitchen—and I grabbed her elbow.

"Why are you with this guy? Is it just to hurt me?"

She shook me off.

"My relationship with Adolf has nothing to do with you. Okay? We're just two people who fell in love."

"Why can't you give me another shot?"

I could tell my voice was slurred, but I couldn't stop myself from talking.

"I won't spend as much time at the studio," I rambled. "I'll be better with your friends. I'm a different person now—I'm more relaxed, more fun—I'm better than this Hitler guy!"

"Seth—"

"I mean, seriously, he's the worst! Why can't everyone see that? How is it just me?"

"Seth!" she hissed. "You're embarrassing yourself."

I looked around. Half the people at the party were staring at me.

"I'm sorry," I murmured.

Anna's fists were clenched; I could tell she was furious at me.

"Please," I begged. "I said I was sorry."

She rolled her eyes.

"Okay," she said, finally. "I forgive you."

The Haunting of 26 Bleecker Street

FATHER CAVALIERI GRIPPED THE banister, waiting for the ache in his chest to pass. His doctor had warned him not to climb any stairs. But he had to keep going. He had a job to do.

He rooted around in his cassock pocket and pulled out a small white pill. He thought of the Eucharist as he laid it on his tongue. After a moment, the pain subsided.

He made his way up the stairs, resting after each flight. At last, he got to Will's apartment.

"Thanks for coming, Father," Will said. "I'm sorry, I should've told you it's a walk-up."

"It is all right, my son," said Father Cavalieri.

He squinted at the haunted youth. His face was smooth and boyish. But his eyes were like an old man's: hollow, sunken, and black. Father Cavalieri had never met him before, but he recognized his face. It was the face of a man who had seen evil.

"Come on in," Will said.

Father Cavalieri stepped into the apartment. There was debris everywhere. Piles of trash, ruined furniture.

"My God," he said. "An evil spirit has laid waste to this place."

"Actually, that's on me," Will said awkwardly. "I've been meaning to clean . . . I just haven't gotten around to it lately."

"Oh."

Will cleared some video game cartridges off the futon so Father Cavalieri could have a place to sit.

"Tell me, my son," said the elderly priest. "What horrors have you seen?"

Will started to answer but was interrupted by a loud whirring noise. His face turned pale as he pointed a trembling finger across the apartment.

Father Cavalieri stood up and squinted. There, on the bathroom sink, lay a pink electric toothbrush. It had turned on by itself and was vibrating loudly, its bristles chafing hard against the porcelain. The priest took out his crucifix and cautiously moved toward the bathroom. He was almost there when the toothbrush suddenly levitated and flew through the air. Father Cavalieri gasped as it whizzed past his head and shattered against a nearby wall. He caught his breath, then sat back down and swallowed another white pill.

"There is a spirit in our midst," he said to Will. "Tell me: has anyone else lived in this place?"

"Just my girlfriend, Liz," Will said. "I mean...my *ex*-girlfriend."

Father Cavalieri sighed. It was just as he'd feared.

"I have seen all this before," he said. "This...'Liz'...she is haunting your apartment."

"That doesn't make any sense," Will said. "I mean, she isn't even dead."

"How do you know?"

Will averted his eyes.

"I've been following her on Twitter," he admitted.

Father Cavalieri nodded wearily.

"She may be alive," he said. "But she will continue to haunt you as long as you still love her."

Will snorted.

"I don't 'still love her,'" he said. "We broke up, like, three months ago. I'm *totally* over her."

"Then why do you still have her toothbrush? What's that about?"

Will swallowed.

"Look," he said. "There's no proof I'm being haunted by Liz. It could be some other spirit."

The TV flipped on suddenly by itself. Father Cavalieri

watched as the poltergeist flicked through the channels settling finally on *America's Next Top Model.* He shot Will a look.

"Okay," Will mumbled. "It's probably Liz."

He covered his face with his hands.

"Why won't she leave me alone?"

"Maybe she has unfinished business," the priest said, "that's keeping her from leaving this realm."

"Well, we never finished watching *The Wire.* We were halfway through season four when we broke up. Do you think that has something to do with it?"

"Possibly," the priest said. He took the *Wire* boxed set off the bookshelf and splashed some holy water onto it.

"Tell me," he said. "What else do you have in this home that belongs to her? Objects can have great talismanic power."

"I don't have any of her stuff," Will said. "I shipped it all to her when we broke up."

Father Cavalieri raised his eyebrows.

"*All* of it?"

Will's face turned red.

"I still have one of her tank tops," he confessed.

"Why do you still have that?" the priest said. "That's really messed up."

"I know."

"What else have you kept?"

"Just a couple random things."

"Show me."

Will reluctantly reached under his bed and pulled out a giant shoe box. It was packed to the brim with Post-it Notes, cards, and photographs. Father Cavalieri took the shoe box, crossed himself, and reached inside. He rooted around in it for a bit and then pulled out a black-and-white photo strip. In the first three pictures, Will and Liz were making funny faces. In the fourth one they were kissing.

"My son," Father Cavalieri said. "You've gotta get rid of this shit."

"I know," Will said. "I will."

"When?"

"Soon."

"Do it right now," the priest commanded. "In front of me."

Will sighed. He grabbed the shoe box, left the apartment, and tossed it down the trash chute in the hall. When he returned, there were tears in his eyes.

"The tank top also," Father Cavalieri said.

"What if she wants it back?" Will asked.

"She's not going to want it back," the priest said. "It's over with her. Just throw it away."

Will opened his underwear drawer and pulled out the neatly folded garment. He stared at it for a moment and then carried it out into the hall. When a few minutes had passed and Will still hadn't returned, Father Cavalieri peeked through the doorway. Will was standing over the trash chute, pressing the tank top to his nose, inhaling its scent.

"Jesus Christ," Father Cavalieri said.

Will jumped up, humiliated.

"Did you just fucking smell it?" the priest asked. "That's, like, the most fucked-up thing I've ever seen."

Will looked down at his feet.

"That was really fucked up," the priest said again.

Will nodded miserably. He took a deep breath, grimaced, and tossed Liz's tank top down the chute.

"Okay," he said when they had returned to the apartment. "That's all her stuff. Will she stop haunting me now?"

"No," the priest said. "There's still something else you must do. One more hurdle in your path to salvation."

"What is it?" Will asked anxiously.

"You must unfriend her on Facebook."

The blood drained from Will's face.

"Now?" he asked, his voice as small as a child's.

"Yes, now," Father Cavalieri said. "Come on, do it."

The priest grabbed Will's computer and handed it to him.

"Be strong," he said.

Will clicked on Liz's profile and moved the cursor toward the "unfriend" icon. His body began to shake.

"I can't," he whispered.

"You *must.*"

Will let out an anguished scream as he slammed his finger down onto the mouse. When Liz's picture vanished, he collapsed onto his knees, weeping into his hands.

"I am proud of you," the priest said.

"Is it over now?" Will asked through his sobs. "Am I free?"

"Almost, my son," the priest said. "There is still one final step."

"You keep saying that!"

"This is the last thing," the priest said. "I promise."

"Okay. What is it?"

"You must sprinkle every wall with holy water, make three signs of the cross... and have sex with someone else."

"What?"

"Have sex with someone else."

Will swallowed.

"Can I just do the first two things?"

"No. In fact, those things aren't even really important. The main thing is you need to start hooking up with people. It's the only way your misery will end."

The priest looked at his watch.

"It's almost ten. I say we pregame here and then go to Floyd."

"I don't know," Will said. "I'm not so good at picking up girls."

"How'd you meet Liz?"

Will smiled nostalgically.

"Well, we were friends for a while before we started dating. And after a couple years, we started to get closer, and soon we were, like, talking for hours on the phone each night—"

Father Cavalieri motioned for him to stop.

"Here," he said, reaching into his cassock pocket. "I'm going to give you a sacred book."

He placed a slim black volume in Will's hands.

"It's called *The Game.* It teaches you how to pick up girls."

Will flipped through the book.

"Peacocking... negging... does this stuff really work?"

The priest nodded solemnly.

"It works."

He opened the fridge, found a six-pack of Pabst, and tossed a can to Will.

"Pound it," he said.

Will cracked open the beer and took a swig.

"Take one of these, too," the priest said, handing him one of his small white pills.

"What is it?"

"Just take it."

Will swallowed the pill, washing it down with the remainder of his beer.

"Nice," the priest said. He grabbed Will's laptop and opened Spotify.

"One song to get us pumped," he said. "And then we're out of here."

He put on something by Santigold. By the time the chorus started, Will had started, reluctantly, to smile.

"There it is!" the priest said, pointing at Will's beaming face. "It's *on*."

He cracked a Pabst and raised it to the heavens.

"A toast," he said. "To moving on."

Will raised his can and laughed.

"Amen," he said.

When Alex Trebek's Ex-Wife Appeared on *Jeopardy!*

CATEGORY: COMMITMENTS

$200

This woman vowed to a game show host that she would "love and cherish him" until the end of time.

$400

This woman, while divorcing a game show host without cause, agreed that she would "remain civil" to him, then went on a political-style campaign to poison all their mutual friends against him.

$600

This game show host generously paid for his ex-wife's divorce lawyers, only to see them gouge him to the brink of ruin.

$800

This game show host used his life savings to fulfill his childhood dream of owning a beach house in Malibu.

$1000

This woman now owns that house.

I Saw Mommy Kissing Santa Claus

I'll never forget the night I saw Mommy kissing Santa Claus. I was only ten years old at the time, but I can still picture it vividly. My mother was standing beneath the mistletoe and Santa was right beside her, a grin on his plump, rosy face. His snow-white beard shone brightly in the moonlight, and when my mother embraced him, his bell-studded coat let out a little jingle.

When I blurted out my secret the next morning, my mother laughed and patted me on the head. But my father remained oddly silent. I could tell by the bags under his eyes that he'd slept terribly. He hadn't touched his breakfast, and his jaw was clenched like a vise.

A few years later, I saw my mother and Santa Claus having sex. My parents were separated by then, but it was still a shock. I was getting a glass of water when I heard a commotion in the rec room. The door was partially open and when I peeked through the crack, I could see them on the couch.

Santa was naked from the waist down, pumping his body into hers. I was horrified, but I couldn't look away. It was just too bizarre. Santa's ass was enormous, I remember, but oddly muscular. His beard was soaked with sweat and I could see flecks of moisture scattering everywhere.

When he was finished, he collapsed on top of her and let out a contented sigh.

"Oh, *Nick,*" my mother said, her fingertips caressing his giant, pale backside.

They lay still for about a minute and then Santa Claus abruptly stood up.

"You have to go already?" my mother said.

"Afraid so," Santa mumbled, as he reclasped his red felt pants.

He stood by the chimney for a moment, his crinkled face flushed from exertion. He was out of shape, clearly, and hadn't yet caught his breath.

"When will I see you again?" my mother asked in a heart-breaking whisper.

"Same time next year," he said. "I promise."

Santa fidgeted uncomfortably. Through a window, I could make out a few elves. They were standing on our front lawn, smoking cigarettes and glancing at their watches.

"Well," he said awkwardly. "Merry Christmas."

I tried my best to forget about the incident—and almost succeeded. But a few years later, when I was back home visiting from college, I saw them together again. They were in the kitchen, staring across the table at each other. There was a plate of milk and cookies between them, but Santa, I noticed, hadn't touched them.

"I just think it's a little odd," my mother was saying. "I mean, you're known for giving presents. It's kind of your thing."

Santa massaged his temples.

"I'm sorry I forgot our anniversary," he said. "What else do you want me to say?"

My mother's eyes welled up with tears.

"Ten years," she said. "We've been doing this for ten years."

She began to sob.

"What *am* I to you?"

"Carolyn..."

"Am I your partner? Or am I just a *whore?*"

"Carolyn!"

They didn't speak for a while. It was so quiet I could hear Santa's reindeer pawing softly at our rooftop. Eventually, my mother reached across the table and took Santa's hand. I could tell she wanted to ask him something, but it took her a while to get the words out.

"Do you still love her?"

"No," he said firmly. "Mrs. Claus and I have a marriage of convenience. I told you that in the beginning."

She squeezed his hand.

"Then why can't you leave her?"

"You wouldn't understand."

She pulled her hand away and folded her arms across her bathrobe.

"It's because of your image, isn't it?"

"It's not because of my image."

"You're afraid of losing the Coke deal."

Santa's eyes narrowed.

"That's a low blow," he said. "That's a real low blow."

"Then what is it?"

"It's everything," Santa said. "The elves, the reindeer. A divorce would devastate them. Look, Carolyn, you know I love you. And I'm going to leave her. I swear. This just isn't the right time."

My mother took a giant swig of eggnog.

"I can't believe this is my life," she said.

"You're being melodramatic."

"Melodramatic? It took you six months to answer my last letter."

"I get a lot of letters."

My mother's nostrils flared with rage. She poured herself another glass of eggnog and downed it in a single swallow.

"I don't know why I love you," she muttered. "It's like some kind of horrible curse. No one deserves to be treated the way you treat me. You kissed me once when I was lonely. So what? Do you realize I've lost everything because of you?"

"You're being irrational."

My mother bit her lip; I could tell she was trying to hold back more tears.

"This ends today," she said softly.

"What?"

"I'm getting out of this thing," she said. "While I still have a tiny shred of dignity left."

Santa Claus rolled his eyes.

"Ho, ho, ho."

"I'm not joking," my mother snapped. "You can cross me off your list, and you don't have to check it twice."

"Sheesh," Santa said. "How long have you had *that* one in your pocket?"

"Get the fuck out of my house," my mother said. "Now."

Santa sighed.

"Can I use the bathroom first?"

"No."

Santa stood up. He leaned across the table and I thought,

for a moment, that he was going to kiss my mother one last time. But he was just reaching for a cookie. He took the biggest one and shoved it in his mouth, spraying crumbs all over his beard.

"Merry fucking Christmas," he said.

It's years later now and I've got a failed marriage of my own. I get the kids every other Christmas and I usually take them over to my mother's. Everyone gets lonely during the holidays, but not like her.

I try not to mention Santa Claus, but on Christmas he inevitably comes up. This last time was my daughter's doing. She's six years old and still not sure whether Santa Claus is real.

"Grandma?" she asked while we were unwrapping the presents. "Do you believe in Santa Claus?"

My mother looked into my daughter's eyes and sighed.

"I used to," she said. "But not anymore."

Man Seeking Woman

You:

You are an intelligent woman, with a sweet and caring soul. You're mature and sophisticated, but you know how to let loose and have a good time. Your first name is Chloe.

Me:

I am a thoughtful, intelligent guy with a sense of humor. I like to stay up late talking about the big questions. I have a large, irremovable tattoo of the word "Chloe" on my chest from a previous relationship.

Invisible Man

THE INVISIBLE MAN WALKED beside his ex-girlfriend. She was obviously on her way to meet someone. He could tell by the way she kept checking her watch and glancing at her reflection in parked cars.

It was possible, he told himself, that she was going to some kind of business function. A job interview, maybe, or drinks with a client. But this sad illusion vanished when she took a left down Greenwich and ducked into a dark Moroccan restaurant.

The invisible man—whose name was David—watched queasily as Kat's date entered. He looked insufferable, a grinning, puffy-faced moron. When he kissed her hello, his lips made a slobbering sound against her face, like someone slurping soup. It was too much for David to take. He headed for the kitchen.

Two chefs were arguing in Spanish. He walked right between them, feeling their hot breath on his face, and found what he was looking for: the wine closet. He knew it was a bad idea to grab a bottle. If the chefs saw him pick one up, they would think the object had levitated. They'd panic and scream and eventually the government would have to come over and vaporize everyone.

"Fuck it," he thought.

He grabbed a '93 Bordeaux, uncorked it, and chugged as much as he could in a single gulp. He glanced at the chefs. Luckily, they weren't looking in his direction.

By the time David got back to Kat's table, she was batting her eyelashes and giggling. He couldn't figure out why until he knelt down on the floor and peeked under the tablecloth. Kat's date was stroking her calf with his foot. David considered punching him in the face. It would be so easy. Just take aim, rear back—and blammo. But then he realized how frightening that would be for Kat. One moment her date is playing footsie with her. The next moment he's screaming in terror as blood shoots insanely out of his nose. He didn't want to put her through that.

Kat went to the bathroom, and her date reached out for the check. David looked over the guy's shoulder while he paid, hoping to catch him tipping poorly. But the guy gave a solid 20 percent. He was a decent person, David realized with misery. Boring, fat, but decent.

David sat cross-legged on the floor, staring up at Kat's date with despair. The guy was humming softly to himself now, drumming his fingers jauntily against the tablecloth. He clearly had high hopes for the rest of his evening. For the first time all night, David wondered if the pair had made love. Somehow, the thought hadn't occurred to him until now.

Eventually, Kat returned to the table. Her makeup looked freshly reapplied.

"Shall we?" she asked.

"We *shall,*" her date responded idiotically.

David sighed and followed them out into the cool September night.

"Well, this was really nice," Kat said.

"Yeah," her date said. "Really nice!"

David rolled his eyes. They were holding hands and swinging their arms back and forth like a couple of fucking teenagers.

David had swiped an open bottle of Merlot on his way out and he was chugging it brazenly, right in the middle of the sidewalk. If somebody walked down Greenwich, they'd see the bottle hovering in midair, its contents disappearing into an invisible void.

"When do I get to see you again?" Kat asked her date.

"The sooner the better," he said.

David smashed the bottle on the ground and the couple swiveled toward him.

"What was that?" Kat asked. She was just a few inches

from David, her sparkling blue eyes looking right through his invisible face.

"It was probably nothing," the date said.

The two of them shared an awkward chuckle.

David looked down the avenue; a cab was coming. This was it, the moment of truth.

"You can have this one," the date said.

"You sure?"

"Of course! Unless . . . you want to get in together."

Kat smiled sweetly at her date, clearly debating whether or not to sleep with him. It was too agonizing for David to watch. He covered his eyes—then remembered that his hands were invisible. He turned around and faced a brick wall.

"I don't know," Kat said. "I should really get back to Brooklyn."

David spun around, smiling with relief. She wasn't going to spend the night with him! She probably never would! This was just a rebound date—a desperate attempt to soothe her loneliness. She still had feelings for him. It was obvious. Their "breakup" was just a bad fight, something they'd laugh about in a few years—or even a few months. They still had a future. David was already visualizing their reconciliation when Kat lunged suddenly at her date and kissed him deeply.

"Tomorrow night," she said. "Let's spend the night together."

David watched in horror as the blushing idiot helped her

into her cab. There was nothing he could do but go back to the base.

By the time David entered the laboratory it was nearly midnight. He drank the antiserum, put on a robe (he'd been naked all night), and entered the conference room. The generals stood as he entered.

"Well?" General Mason asked breathlessly. "Did you find Mahmoud?"

David sighed. He'd been assigned to track a terrorist and, if possible, eliminate him. He'd intended to look for the guy but had gotten somewhat sidetracked.

"I couldn't find him," he lied.

The president of the United States buried his face in his hands.

"Then all is lost," he said.

The generals and the president spoke for a while in hushed tones. An attack was coming, something having to do with bombs or missiles or something. David wasn't paying attention. He was pretty drunk.

"We have one more ounce of serum," a scientist was saying. "That's three more hours of invisibility..."

David thought back to his final talk with Kat. She'd complained that he'd been distant. But what did she expect? He worked for a top secret wing of the CIA. He'd shared more with her than anyone on earth. His own parents thought he was a dentist. Someone nudged him politely on the shoulder; when he looked up, he realized that the president was staring at him.

"Sorry," he said. "Must've zoned out." He shook his head. "My girlfriend, she broke up with me last month. One day everything was fine and then all of a sudden—boom. It's like, if I was doing something wrong, she could've told me and I would've tried to fix it. I would've made an effort, you know? But she didn't even give me a chance."

There was a long pause.

"Agent Five," the president said. "We've spent decades perfecting invisibility technology. Four good agents have died. The serum is matched to your DNA; that means we can't replace you on this mission. If you don't catch Mahmoud tomorrow, thousands will die, perhaps millions. Can our nation count on you or not?"

David shrugged.

"I guess."

The invisible man followed Kat to La Boulange. She'd referred to it once as "our place." Now it was *their* place: her and Kurt Parrola's.

It hadn't been easy finding the guy's name; David had had to slip one of his hairs into a DNA scanner and run the enzymes through the government's secret people-tracker. After that, he'd spent six hours on Google.

Kurt was thirty-one—the same age as he was—and worked for some kind of nonprofit. He'd gone to Wesleyan and occasionally took improvisational comedy classes at the Upright Citizens Brigade Theatre. David feared that he was rich.

His invisible earpiece buzzed.

"Have you located Mahmoud?" General Mason demanded.

"Uh-huh," David mumbled absently. Kat was feeding Kurt a bite of chocolate cake. She was literally spooning it into his mouth like he was a fucking child. What the fuck was this? What the fuck was going on?

"You have executive authority to assassinate Mahmoud," the general was saying. "By whatever force necessary."

"Yeah," David said. "He's here."

The general sighed.

"Agent Five," he said. "If you don't take out Mahmoud in the next two hours, he's going to carry out his attacks and..."

David took out his earpiece, tired of the distraction. Kat and Kurt were getting up to leave. If he was going to do something, he had to act now.

Kat kissed Kurt on the nose.

"Let's go back to my place," she whispered.

"Sounds good to me," Kurt said, clumsily hooking his arm around her back. David watched with horror as his hand drifted lower and lower before settling on her buttock. He gave it a proprietary squeeze and grinned at her.

"I'll be right back," he said.

He strolled toward the bathroom, humming softly to himself. David followed close behind.

Kurt was calmly relieving himself when he felt a hand clamp down on his shoulder.

"What the fuck!" he shouted, spraying urine all over his hands. "What the fuck!"

"Kurt Parrola," David said. "You're having a schizophrenic break."

Kurt swiveled his head around in a panic.

"Who's talking?"

"I'm a voice inside your head," David continued. "You've gone completely insane."

He hiccupped a few times. He'd been drinking since noon and was very drunk.

"You should go to a hospital."

Kurt looked helplessly around the bathroom, his eyes wide with terror.

"What is this? Who's talking?"

David picked up a roll of toilet paper and waved it around. Kurt gasped at the sight of the hovering object.

"This isn't real," Kurt whispered to himself. "This isn't real!"

He began to cry, and David felt his first spasm of guilt. But he pressed on, fueled by drunkenness and envy.

"The voices will continue," he continued, "unless you go to a hospital, commit yourself, and—"

There was a knock on the door.

"Sweetie?" Kat said. "Are you all right?"

David gasped. He couldn't see his reflection in the mirror, but he could sense that he'd turned pale.

"No," Kurt murmured. "Something's happened to me . . . I think I'm sick!"

Before David could move out of the way, Kat shoved open the door. The knob smacked into his tailbone and he let out an involuntary curse.

"Fuck!"

Kat's eyes widened.

"David?"

David bit his tongue, trying his best to keep as still as possible.

"David, are you in here?"

"Who's David?" Kurt asked.

"My ex-boyfriend," Kat explained. "David, I know you're here! I heard you!"

David sighed.

"I'm sorry," he murmured.

Kat kicked the door with anger.

"I can't believe you'd follow us like this!" she shouted. "You asshole—you were trying to make him think he'd gone crazy, weren't you?"

David sighed again.

"I'm sorry," he repeated.

"Un-fucking-believable. You're drunk, too, aren't you?"

"No!" David shouted, a little too loudly.

"You *swore* you would never spy on me. When you told me about the serum, you swore you would never use it on me!"

"Well, *you* swore you would never tell anyone about the serum! And now you've told Kurt!"

"What the fuck was I supposed to do? Let him think he'd gone insane?"

Kurt fell to the floor, sobbing uncontrollably. His pants were around his ankles. Kat knelt down beside him and gently rubbed his shoulders.

"Honey," she said. "It's okay. My ex is in the CIA—"

"That's top secret information," David interrupted.

"Oh, fuck you!" she snapped.

She rubbed Kurt's back and whispered in his ear.

"There's nothing wrong with you—my ex is just a jealous, pathetic jerk."

"I'm sorry," David muttered for what felt like the thousandth time of the night. "I still love you."

Kat rolled her eyes.

"Come on," she said to Kurt. "Let's go."

"I'm sick!" he cried.

Kat sneered in David's general direction.

"See what you've done? I'm going to have to give him a Valium or something."

She swung open the door and helped Kurt out of the bathroom. David watched as the couple shuffled toward the door, their arms around each other. Just before they left the restaurant, Kat swung her arms wildly in a circle to make sure David wasn't still following them. Then she took her new boyfriend by the hand and led him out into the night.

David got back to the lab about an hour later. The generals were huddled in a corner, speaking in whispers.

"Washington is lost," one said. "And Chicago will never be 'Chicago' again."

General Mason was staring at a map of the United States. Every few minutes, an underling whispered something into his ear and he solemnly crossed off the name of a major city.

The president was sitting in a folding chair while a woman applied makeup to his face.

"Which would you prefer to say?" a speechwriter asked him. "'Atrocity' or 'tragedy'?"

"'Atrocity,'" the president said.

The makeup woman finished powdering the president's face and he opened his eyes.

"Ah," he said, recognizing David. "Agent Five. I'm sorry things didn't go as planned."

David nodded. He was thinking about the first time he met Kat, at a bar near the Pentagon. He hadn't even planned on going out that night; he'd just put in a sixteen-hour shift. But some voice in his head made him go out for a beer—and Kat had been right there, in a shiny red dress, like a gift-wrapped present from God. He'd sung out loud on his way home. He could remember thinking, very distinctly, that he would probably never be so happy again. It turned out he'd been right.

"It's not your fault," the president said. "You did all you could."

David's eyes welled up with tears as the old man squeezed his shoulder.

"A new day will come," the president said. "You'll see."

But David knew better.

It was the end of the fucking world.

The Present

I DON'T UNDERSTAND," Professor Xander Kaplan said while his girlfriend sobbed into a pillow. "I thought you liked tulips."

"I *do,*" she said. "It's just...you get them for me every year. It's starting to get a little impersonal. I mean, this time you didn't even include a *card.*"

Xander winced. Her reasoning was sound.

"I apologize," he said. "I obviously made an error in judgment."

He tried to take her hand, but she pulled it out of reach.

"Do you remember what I did for *your* birthday?" she said. "I got you that new Bunsen burner you wanted. I knit you a pair of wool socks so your feet wouldn't get cold in the lab."

She covered her face with her hands.

"You never make that kind of effort for me!" she cried. "All you do is think about yourself."

"That's incorrect," Xander said defensively. "What about

emiladium? It took me nine months to synthesize that element, and I named it after you."

"You were going to synthesize that element anyway," Emily said. "You needed it for your 'secret project'—that silver orb thing in your lab. Emiladium wasn't about me. It was about *you*. I mean, for God's sake, you won't even tell me what it *does*."

Xander sighed. She'd made an excellent argument.

"Is there anything I can do to make it up to you?" he asked.

Emily blinked back some tears.

"I don't know," she said. "I mean... it's not like you can just *go back in time* and get me a different present."

Xander's expression brightened.

"Wait there," he said, leaping to his feet. "I'll be right back!"

Xander hurried down the hall, crept into his laboratory, and locked the door behind him. His time machine was right where he had left it.

He climbed inside the silver orb and flicked on the power switch. His plan was simple: travel back in time to this morning, find a new gift for Emily, and bring it to the present. But there were a couple of risks. There was a chance, for example, that using the machine would cause the universe to explode. (He'd never tested the thing out before.) There was also no guarantee that he would be able to find a good present. He only had enough emiladium to fuel five minutes of time travel. That didn't give him a lot of "wiggle room." Wherever he went, he'd have to shop efficiently.

Xander was usually a pretty good problem solver. (He had, for example, invented a time machine.) But quantum physics and nuclear hydraulics were trivial compared to the rigors of gift shopping. He massaged his temples, trying to remember if Emily had dropped any hints lately. He vaguely recalled her staring at a vase in Crate & Barrel. But that place was full of vases. There was no way he'd be able to pick out the right one.

He was trying to remember the name of her favorite perfume when a thought entered his head: maybe he was thinking too small? His machine could transport him to any time and place in human history. Why go back a few hours when he could go back a few centuries?

He knew Emily loved Shakespeare. She'd written her senior thesis on one of his tragedies. Why not travel back to the Globe Theatre and swipe her an original script? It wouldn't be too difficult, he reasoned. All he'd have to do was dash backstage and grab one. It would be the most impressive gift she'd ever received in her life!

But which tragedy had Emily written her thesis about? He knew it was one of the king ones. Richard the something or Charles the something. But there were a bunch of those. What if he got it wrong? It was too risky.

There was always jewelry. He knew the general construction dates for Tut's tomb. He could park in front of the pyramid, run inside, and snatch a jadestone. Some Hebrew slaves would probably chase after him, but as soon as he made it back into his orb, he'd be home free. He entered in the coordinates and was about to push the lever when he started to second-guess himself again. Buying women jewelry was always chancy. Emily had very specific tastes. What if she didn't like jade? It wasn't like he'd be able to go back and return it.

He thought back to the night they met. He was finishing his PhD at the time and his lab had closed early because of Easter. He'd stuffed his papers into his briefcase and shuffled through the rain to the 116th Street station. It was 4:05 a.m. and the platform was deserted, except for Emily. It had been several days since Xander's last conversation with a human. And when she started to speak to him, he felt the stirrings of a panic attack. But Emily's friendly smile managed somehow to put him at ease. She was awfully cheerful, given her circumstances. Her MetroCard had expired, she said, and the machines were broken. She'd been stranded for over twenty minutes. Would he be willing to sell her a ride? Xander nodded and watched as she rooted around in her purse for some cash to pay him back. It was a minute or two before it occurred to him that she had given him a chance to be gallant.

"You don't have to reimburse me," he said. "I'll swipe you in for free."

She thanked him enthusiastically and then—shockingly—wrapped her arms around his torso. Xander wasn't used to physical contact, and although the hug was brief, it caused his entire body to tingle, from head to toe. It was a startling sensation, like walking through an electrically charged field. He still felt that way whenever she touched him.

Xander was an atheist and believed fiercely in random causality. But by the end of their shared subway ride, he was sure he'd experienced a miracle. This wonderful person had shown up out of nowhere and given him a chance at love.

And in return, he'd given her three years of misery. He thought about all of his Saturday nights at the lab, ignoring her calls, making excuses. He thought about the way she'd cried when he handed her the tulips.

How could he make up for three years of romantic ineptitude with a single birthday present?

Maybe the solution was simpler than he thought. There were a pencil and pad on his desk. He could go back a few hours and spend the morning writing her a card. He would tell her in a plainly worded note how much he loved her—how much gratitude he felt whenever he saw her smiling face.

But Xander wasn't much of a writer. His sentences would come out poorly, he knew, like the wooden prose of his grant proposals. It was pointless to even try.

He closed his eyes and concentrated. There had to be a right answer.

Cleopatra's crown.

Joan of Arc's sword.

A baby dinosaur.

What was the greatest thing he could give her, the very best present in the world? It was the hardest problem he'd ever attempted to solve.

But then, as always, the solution came to him.

Xander parked his time machine on 116th Street and dashed into the subway. It was 3:45 a.m., a little over three years in the past.

Emily was standing by the turnstile, swiping and reswiping her expired MetroCard. It took Xander a moment to recognize her. In his memories, she'd worn a tight angora sweater and bright red lipstick. But in reality, she'd been dressed more casually. A T-shirt, a raincoat, and jeans.

He took a deep breath and approached her.

"Let me guess," he said. "Expired MetroCard."

She chuckled.

"How'd you know?"

"I had a hunch," he said. "Come on, I'll swipe you through."

"That's okay," she said. "I'll just go to the machine upstairs or—"

"The machines are all broken," he said, cutting her off.

He could hear a train approaching in the distance.

"You better catch this one," he said. "The next won't come for another twenty minutes."

Before she could protest, he took out his MetroCard and swiped her through the turnstile.

She smiled back at him with confusion.

"Aren't you coming?" she asked as the train pulled into the station.

Xander averted his eyes. He was worried that if he looked at her he would start to cry.

"I need to take a different train," he said.

"Well, at least let me pay you for the—"

"That's all right," he said, his voice breaking. "It's a present."

He was about to turn away when she leaned over the turnstile and hugged him. It was exactly as he remembered it, her long brown hair brushing softly against his neck, his entire body tingling with warmth.

"Thanks!" she said.

He tried to say "You're welcome," but the words got caught in his throat. He waved good-bye as she boarded the train. Then he marched out of the station alone.

Children of the Dirt

ACCORDING TO ARISTOPHANES, there were originally three sexes: the Children of the Moon (who were half male and half female), the Children of the Sun (who were fully male), and the Children of the Earth (who were fully female). Everyone had four legs, four arms, and two heads and spent their days in blissful contentment.

Zeus became jealous of the humans' joy, so he decided to split them all in two. Aristophanes called this punishment the Origin of Love. Because ever since, the Children of the Earth, Moon, and Sun have been searching the globe in a desperate bid to find their other halves.

Aristophanes's story, though, is incomplete. Because there was also a fourth sex: the Children of the Dirt. Unlike the other three sexes, the Children of the Dirt consisted of just one half. Some were male and some were female and each had just two arms, two legs, and one head.

The Children of the Dirt found the Children of the Earth, Moon, and Sun to be completely insufferable. Whenever they saw a two-headed creature walking by, talking to itself in baby-talk voices, it made them want to vomit. They hated going to parties and when there was no way to get out of one they sat in the corner, too bitter and depressed to talk to anybody. The Children of the Dirt were so miserable that they invented wine and art to dull their pain. It helped a little, but not really. When Zeus went on his rampage, he decided to leave the Children of the Dirt alone. "They're already fucked," he explained.

Happy gay couples descend from the Children of the Sun, happy lesbian couples descend from the Children of the Earth, and happy straight couples descend from the Children of the Moon. But the vast majority of humans are descendants of the Children of the Dirt. And no matter how long they search the Earth, they'll never find what they're looking for. Because there's nobody for them, not anybody in the world.

Trade

BEN HAD ALWAYS KNOWN, on some level, that it was possible for him to get traded. He'd seen it happen to dozens of guys over the years, including some of his closest friends. It was part of the game. Still, he had never been traded himself and he was having some trouble accepting it. He kept expecting someone to tap him on the shoulder and tell him the whole thing was a joke.

"Here's your stuff," Hailey said, dropping a duffel bag at his feet. "Good-bye."

Ben stared at her for a moment, expecting some kind of encouragement or sympathy. But Hailey just stood there.

"So that's it, then," Ben said. "After three and a half years."

"What do you want me to say?" Hailey snapped.

He picked up the bag and slung it wearily over his shoulder. There was nothing he could do. When your girlfriend decides to trade you, that's it. You're through.

"I just don't get it!" Ben shouted over the din of the jukebox. "I thought things were going really well."

"They weren't," his brother, Craig, informed him. "The writing was on the wall."

"Really?"

"Oh, yeah. Your record's been sinking all year. You told me yourself you had a five-argument losing streak. And then there were all those errors."

Ben nodded ruefully. There *had* been a lot of errors this year. Forty-five Missed Compliments, three Forgotten Events, twelve Accidental Insults—he'd been playing like a rookie.

Craig squeezed his little brother's shoulder.

"I'm sorry, Ben," he said. "Believe me, I know what you're going through. Remember in oh-four-oh-five? When Zoe traded me?"

Ben nodded. They'd come to the same bar then.

"I was devastated," Craig said. "I'd just taken her to Henry's Inn for her birthday—you know, that fancy place with all the candles? Got her a steak, gave her a necklace, took her to a show, massaged her feet..."

"You hit for the *cycle?*"

"Uh-huh. Then I wake up the next day and she's giving me my marching orders. Tells me she needs to 'shake things up' if she wants to remain a contender."

"Unbelievable."

"It was right before Valentine's Day."

Ben nodded.

"The Trade Deadline."

"Exactly. You know what the worst part is? I *know* the guy she traded me for. And he's garbage."

"Really?"

"Yeah, he's some kind of banker. Always looking at himself in the mirror and fixing his goddamn tie. It's like, 'Come on, you traded me for *this* guy?' I mean, okay, his stats are pretty good. He's got me beat in Money—and his Sex Numbers are pretty impressive. But what about intangibles? What about attitude? Intelligence? Effort? Those things gotta count for something!"

He ate some potato chips and wiped the grease off on his jeans.

"Who am I kidding?" he muttered. "These days? The only thing they care about is the bottom line."

When Hailey offered Ben his contract, he was so excited that he barely bothered to read it. He realized now that he should have perused the fine print. According to the Trade Clause, he had seventy-two hours to get his stuff out of her apartment.

After that, he wouldn't be allowed to set foot in her home. His Sexual Privileges were revoked, along with Hugging Rights and Injury Sympathy. It was insane. Why had he given her so much power in the first place?

He was struggling to get through the clause on Mutual Friends—the footnotes alone were five pages—when he heard a loud knock on the door. He took a long, slow breath and opened it.

Hailey's new boyfriend smirked down at him. He had tattoos on his neck and was wearing a scarf and shades, even though it was summer and he was indoors.

"'Sup," he said.

Ben forced a smile. There was no reason to be impolite. It was an awkward situation—but what could he do about it?

"'Sup," he responded.

The two men shook hands, reached into their pockets, and exchanged keys.

"This one's for Hailey's lobby," Ben explained. "And this one's for her door. You have to kind of push it in and then twist."

The tattooed man nodded.

"Lisa likes it from behind," he offered.

Ben nodded awkwardly.

"Okay," he said. "I guess that's it, then."

"Good luck."

"You too."

"What do you mean, an artist?" Craig asked. "Like, in advertising or something?"

Ben swallowed. It was taking him a tremendous amount of effort to get his words out. It was like his tongue was coated with clay.

"He does performance art," he mumbled. "Based on Camus... and Sartre."

"Jesus," Craig said. "I can't believe she traded you for *that*."

He ordered them another round of drinks.

"Is it all finalized?"

Ben nodded.

"We both passed our physicals."

He banged his fist against the bar.

"Damn it!" he said. "I know I'm not an *all-star,* all right? My job is boring, I spend too much time doing crossword puzzles, and I like bad TV. I just... I thought I was worth *something.*"

He shook his head.

"She must have really wanted to get rid of me."

A mousy girl with glasses opened the door and looked Ben up and down.

"Is now a good time?" he asked.

"Sure," she said, her voice a little shaky. "Come on in."

He laid his bag down neatly on the rug and looked around. Her apartment was a lot smaller than Hailey's, but at least the TV was bigger.

"Is that a plasma?"

Lisa laughed.

"Keanu said it was making him stupid. It was one of our biggest fights."

Ben nodded.

"Hailey hated TV. Especially my favorite show."

"*Jersey Shore,* right?"

Ben winced.

"I didn't know that showed up in the stats."

She held up a copy of his old contract.

"Everything's in here."

Ben held his breath while she adjusted her glasses and flipped through the pages.

"You really should have negotiated for more," she said. "I know you were just a draft pick, but this is ridiculous."

"What do you mean? It's not a good deal?"

"It's terrible. I mean, look at this. Your Sexual Privileges are almost nonexistent."

Ben sighed. He had always suspected Hailey had screwed him with that clause—but he didn't have any other long-term contracts to compare it to, and he'd been too embarrassed to ask his brother if it was normal.

"And this Emotional Support clause is pathetic. One Career Pep Talk a year?"

"That's low?"

"*Yes*. Girlfriends are usually required to give at least one a month. Why didn't you hire a lawyer?"

Ben threw up his hands in frustration.

"Because I'm an idiot," he said. "Because I'm a worthless idiot."

He picked up his duffel bag.

"You know, you don't have to take me," he said. "I know there's a release clause. You can just put me on waivers."

Lisa laughed.

"Why would I put you on waivers? I traded for you."

"What do you mean?"

"The trade was *my* idea."

Ben slowly put his bag back down.

"It was?"

"Yes! I mean... Hailey didn't exactly argue when I made the offer. But I set the whole thing up. I don't have a lot of relationship experience, but I can spot a good deal when I see it."

Ben felt a swelling in his throat. He realized he was about to cry.

"You think I'm a good deal?"

She flipped through his contract.

"Sure," she said. "I mean, some of your stats are low. Like . . . these Sex Numbers. It's something to work on."

Ben nodded.

"But your crossword skills are through the roof. You've got a solid job. Great taste in TV."

She leaned forward and kissed him on the lips.

"And you're cute."

"I am?"

"*I* think so."

She crumpled up his old agreement and tossed it in a wastebasket.

"But that thing is ridiculous. I can't hold you to it."

"Seriously?"

"Yeah—I'd feel like a monster."

He was so grateful he grabbed her hand and pressed it to his lips. She giggled.

"But wait," he said. "What are we going do about a contract?"

She ran her fingers through his hair. Then she reached into her pocket and pulled out a blank piece of paper.

"Let's start from scratch," she said.

He wrapped his arms around her, laughing with relief. There was nothing like joining a new team; there was nothing like Opening Day.

Acknowledgments

This book would not exist without the support, advice, and encouragement of Daniel Greenberg, the best book agent on earth! I feel so incredibly lucky to have him in my corner. I also want to thank my wonderful editors, Reagan Arthur and Laura Tisdel, for devoting so much time and care to these stories. Their skilled edits (and judicious cuts) drastically improved this collection.

Thanks to everyone at Serpent's Tail, especially Rebecca Gray and Anna-Marie Fitzgerald, for continuing to believe in my writing, even as it gets increasingly weird. And thanks to Susan Morrison and David Remnick, for letting me write for *The New Yorker.*

Brent Katz, a fantastic writer and friend, came up with the title for this book. He also pitched me over a dozen "backups," some of which are too good not to print here. My three favorites:

1. *Cupid Kills Himself*

2. *Men Are from Brooklyn, Women Are from Brooklyn*
3. *Love in the Time of HPV*

Alex Woo nodded politely when I cornered him once at a party and ranted for an hour about the general concept of this book. And Jake Luce, as always, provided valuable insight at every step of my writing process.

I know next to nothing about science but stubbornly insist on writing about it. Luckily, I'm friends with the brilliant (and patient) Pat Swieskowski. He always takes the time to talk to me when I call him with questions about "chemicals and robot stuff." If it weren't for him, these stories would be even more ridiculous.

The story "Wishes" shares a premise with a failed sketch I wrote with Bryan Tucker back in 2009. Thank you, Bryan, for letting me recycle it here!

My biggest influence while writing this book was *69 Love Songs*, the landmark Magnetic Fields album composed by Stephin Merritt. Other artists I've ripped off include T. C. Boyle, Stanley Elkin, and Matt Groening.

Thank you, Mom, Dad, Alex, Nat, and Michael for your love and support.

And thanks also to: Christoph Niemann, Matthew Schoch, Marlena Bittner, Deborah Jacobs, Michael Pietsch, Andrew Steele, Rachel Goldenberg, Dan Abramson, Lorne Michaels,

Steve Higgins, Marika Sawyer, John Mulaney, Seth Meyers, Farley Katz, Monica Padrick, Lee Eastman, Gregory McKnight, Keith Sears, Mary Coleman, Pete Docter, Jonas Rivera, and Wikipedia.

Most of all, though, I want to thank my beautiful, brilliant, magical girlfriend Kathleen, who inspired all the best parts of this book. I love you.

About the Author

Simon Rich is the author of *Ant Farm, Free-Range Chickens, Elliot Allagash,* and *What in God's Name.* He has written for *The New Yorker, McSweeney's, Saturday Night Live,* and Pixar. He lives in Brooklyn.